TAGGART CASEBOOK

GEOFF TIBBALLS

SCOTTISH TELEVISION ENTERPRISES

BOXTREE

ACKNOWLEDGEMENTS

The author would like to thank the following for helping him with his
enquiries: Iain Anders, Chris Bell, Harriet Buchan, Glenn Chandler,
Anita Cox, Neil Duncan, Blythe Duff, Fiona Harvey, Robert Love,
Stephen McCrossan, Mark McManus, Annette MacMillan,
James Macpherson, Robert Robertson and Boxtree editor Katy Carrington.
Photographs by Paul Bonatti.

First published in Great Britain in 1994 by Boxtree Limited

1 3 5 7 9 10 8 6 4 2

Designed by Martin Lovelock
Printed and bound in Great Britain by the
Bath Press Group, Glasgow, for
Boxtree Limited
Broadwall House
21 Broadwall
London SE1 9PL

A CIP catalogue entry for this book is available from the British Library.

ISBN: 1 85283 926 0

Jacket photographs courtesy of Scottish Television Enterprises

CONTENTS

DEDICATION

The death of Mark McManus on 6 June 1994 left a gap in many people's lives. Not only those of us who worked with him from day to day and knew him as a friend and colleague but also members of the public to whom he was more than just an actor. For Mark, like Taggart, was a man of the people. He was proud of his Glasgow roots and didn't want to throw them away. He didn't get grand and starry. He saw the public as his friends, unless they demonstrated otherwise, and they in turn reciprocated the feeling. He enjoyed being recognized and chatted to by the punters who stopped to watch us filming, and was only too happy to sign autographs. When he died, people felt they had lost one of their own.

I once said that Mark McManus *was* Taggart but really that was a cliché. He was not the wee, hard man as was often claimed but a very nice, private, rather quiet person. He was an avid reader and always had a book in his hand. We had requests to take paperbacks to him in hospital and I remember the last time I saw him there he was reading a book.

Although *Taggart* was his crowning glory, people tended to forget that Mark had done so many different things before. I think it was only when he died that the full extent of his acting career came to be acknowledged. As well as the Australian tour of *Half a Sixpence*, the film *Ned Kelly* with Mick Jagger and television series such as *Sam*, *The Brothers* and *Strangers*, he also had a run of roles at the National Theatre. Probably his most memorable performance at the National Theatre was as Jesus in the promenade-style *Passion Plays*.

Mark had a good sense of humour and that came over in his playing of Jim Taggart. Indeed, he would often make suggestions to give a particular line a humourous slant. One hang-up he did have was about learning character names. Scenes at the station invariably involved the mention of many characters and half-way through a speech, you could be sure he would forget the names and explode with frustration. Having said that, it was very rarely that we had to do a retake for Mark. He was a consummate professional who was never late and always well-prepared. It was only in the final months, after the death of his wife Marion, that he found it hard to summon up enthusiasm.

Over the years, a number of guest stars appeared in the *Taggart* stories: people like Isla Blair, Jill Gascoine, Annette Crosbie, Ann Mitchell and Hannah Gordon. Mark always behaved towards them with great courtesy and friendliness – not something that can be said of every leading actor in a television series. Many phoned us to express their concern about his health and wish him well. We even received a bouquet of flowers from TV New Zealand, a mark of his popularity out there.

He was held in great affection by his co-stars, James Macpherson and Blythe Duff, both of whom felt that they had learned so much from him. James often said that Mark had a quality of stillness and an economy of technique that many actors might envy. Mark also did a lot for police recruitment, crime prevention campaigns and police charities. Strathclyde police were out in strength for his funeral and saluted his coffin as it was carried out. It was a moving moment.

I know I speak for everyone involved in *Taggart* when I say it has been a privilege and a pleasure to have worked with Mark for the last twelve years. We are all very grateful for the memory. I suspect the viewers feel much the same.

ROBERT LOVE, EXECUTIVE PRODUCER.

1

THE INVESTIGATION BEGINS

Writer Glenn Chandler was wandering through Glasgow's Maryhill cemetery in search of inspiration for the new three-part detective thriller which he had been commissioned to write. He looked around at the names on the headstones and spotted one which caught his imagination. It was for a member of a family by the name of Taggart.

Glenn thought to himself: 'Taggart. That rings true.'

Ever since, the name of Taggart has been synonymous with quality drama, presenting intricate murder mysteries in the finest traditions of the whodunit, all set against the gritty, realistic background of modern Glasgow.

It was in the early Eighties that Robert Love, Controller of Drama at Scottish Television (STV), hit upon the idea of making a series about a Glasgow detective. As one of the smaller ITV companies, STV often had difficulty in persuading the network to accept its programmes. Robert Love's solution was simple. 'I wanted to find something that the network couldn't refuse from a regional company such as ourselves.'

His other mission was to find new writers for television. 'In my first three years with STV, from 1980, I had tried out new writers in a series of half-hour, low-budget studio plays called *Preview*. One of the writers to emerge from *Preview* was Glenn Chandler, who had hitherto had most of his attempts to become a television writer rejected. He had written for the theatre and I had been told about him by an actor who had appeared in one of his plays at the Soho Poly, a lunchtime theatre in London. I made contact with Glenn and he wrote one of the plays for *Preview*.'

The first play Glenn Chandler wrote for *Preview* was called 'The Horseman's Word'. Glenn says: 'It was about the secret society of Horsemen which exists in various parts of Scotland – a bit like the Masons. An old Aberdeenshire journalist told me all about the initiation ceremony.'

Incidentally, small sections of 'The Horseman's Word' have been incorporated into the 1994 *Taggart* Hallowe'en special, 'Hellfire'.

Glenn ended up writing three plays for *Preview* and began getting commissions from elsewhere, notably the BBC hospital drama *Angels* and the long-running *Crown Court* from Granada. 'It was *Crown Court* which inspired my interest in crime,' says Glenn. 'To research it, I thought I'd better go and sit in a courtroom. So I went to the Old Bailey and found it intriguing. Then I went to a secondhand bookshop and bought *The Murderer and the Trial* by Edgar Lustgarten, which retold famous old cases. I was hooked – and my fascination with crime has never wavered since.'

Nurturing his idea for a television detective, and wanting a new writer rather than an established one because he thought that way he would get a fresher response, Robert Love decided to approach Glenn Chandler. Glenn recalls: 'Robert invited me to lunch in Covent Garden. I'd never been to Covent Garden in my life and I wore my kilt – the first time I'd worn it in public for years! It must have brought me good luck because he asked me whether I would do this three-hour mini-series about a Glasgow detective.

'Right from the start, I had Mark McManus in mind to play my central character. He was the only actor I could think of who would be suitable, and I

Jim Taggart and Peter Livingstone in the first ever **Taggart** episode, 'Killer'.

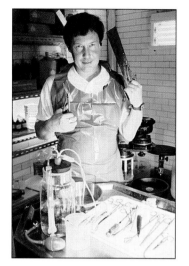

Glenn Chandler,
the creator of
Taggart, gets to
grips with the tools
of his trade.

felt I had to have somebody in my head when I was writing it.'

Glenn's other principal character was Peter Livingstone. Robert Love says: 'We decided to make Livingstone very different from Taggart. Taggart is a Glaswegian born and bred – he has come up through the ranks, he is a man of the people. Livingstone, on the other hand, was one of the new breed of policemen. He was a middle-class boy, doing a job of which his parents didn't approve. He was a graduate and, worse than that, he came from Edinburgh! Taggart likes to dismiss Edinburgh as "one street and a clock made out o' flowers!"

'We actually made a big mistake with that first script. Glenn wrote the first episode, which was very good. But when I read the second, I immediately became concerned because I realized the story would not hold up for three episodes.

'I thought, how do I tell him this? Because obviously he had put a lot of work into it. But I rang him up and said: "I've got something terrible to tell you."

'He said: "It's OK, I know. It's not going to work." He had come to the same conclusion as me.

'Time was running out on us. We had promised to deliver to the network by a certain date. We were supposed to be making our three-parter at the start of 1983 and here we were in the previous October without a workable script.

'So Glenn had to go straight back to the drawing-board and this time, before writing the actual script, he produced a full outline for all three episodes in great detail. It is a rule to which we have adhered ever since. You could say it was a lesson learned.'

The result was 'Killer'. That first story was not called 'Taggart' simply because, at that stage, nobody had the slightest idea that the series would still be running eleven years later. It was only after 'Killer' was shown to immense critical acclaim that the ITV network decided it wanted more.

Robert Love had also considered Mark McManus for the role of Taggart. 'We needed an actor who was an authentic Glaswegian and who was recognizable to the audience at large – not just a Scottish audience. We needed a "face". Mark fitted the bill perfectly. He had been in high-profile series such as *Sam* and *The Brothers*, and at the time was playing Detective Chief Superintendent Lambie, the desk man in *Strangers*, the programme which popularized Don Henderson's Bulman character. But it was because he was doing Lambie that we nearly didn't approach him. I was afraid that people might think we were simply transferring the character from one show to another, even though Lambie was totally different to Taggart.

'The other reason we very nearly didn't cast Mark was that, in those days, the minimum height for policemen in the Glasgow force was six foot. And Mark was only five foot nine. The minimum height has since been lowered considerably but at that time we thought that, in order to be strictly accurate, our Taggart should be a tall man. So we went through a list of other possible candidates – but we kept coming back to Mark.'

The actor did not take much persuading. 'I was living in London at the time,' remembered Mark, 'and working at the National Theatre. The script for "Killer" arrived through the door and I read it on the train that morning on my way to the theatre. I got off the train at St Pancras, rang Robert Love and said: "It's for me." I thought, if ever there was something for me, this was it. Coming from Glasgow myself, the whole thing struck a chord. Funnily enough, I had rarely played a Scotsman before. Lambie was Scottish, but even he wasn't a Glaswegian.'

Jim Taggart has become a Glasgow folk hero. Everyone in the city seems to know him. Such is the show's realism that Mark McManus once admitted: 'In some pubs in Glasgow, they still dash out the back door when I walk in 'cos they think I'm one of the bizzies!'

The police love Taggart too. With a face hewn out of granite, he is hard-working and as straight as they come and possesses that delicious black humour which can produce a wry comment from the most gruesome scene.

'There has always been a good deal of black humour in *Taggart*,' says Robert Love. 'It's very important to the show. The thing about Taggart as a person is that people can identify with him. He's not perfect, he's a bit surly sometimes, life gets on top of him, but his heart's in the right place. And, above all, he's a good detective.'

Robert Love, executive producer of the series.

The supporting characters have also been vital components in the *Taggart* success story. For the first two stories, Taggart's boss was Superintendent Robert Murray, known to all as 'The Mint'. He was then replaced by the redoubtable Jack McVitie, not-so-affectionately christened 'The Biscuit'. Taggart and he have little in common (Taggart is not one for public relations and games of golf) but beneath the surface friction, the two men have a healthy respect for each other. Even so, Taggart usually gets far more help and support from the amiable police pathologist, Dr Stephen Andrews.

It was Glenn Chandler's idea to put Taggart's wife, Jean, in a wheelchair, a position to which she was confined as a result of complications during the

birth of their daughter Alison. 'I wanted to put the wife in a wheelchair to make her vulnerable,' says Glenn. 'She was writing a book on how disabled people have sex and a lot of people thought Taggart was the murderer in "Killer" because he wasn't getting any at home!'

'Jean is a very dynamic character,' adds Robert Love, 'a good sounding-board for Taggart. There was a nice moment in one episode where Taggart was having serious doubts as to whether he would be able to solve the case and she said: "You will. You always do." This was just before they turned the lights off in bed – it was a timely boost to his morale.

'We wanted to depict Jean as a very independent-minded person – she has taken a university degree, had her book published and travelled to Canada – one who would take no stick from Taggart. She gives as good as she gets. Fundamentally, they have a very good relationship. They're devoted to one another, although, as with most couples, it doesn't always show. Take "Evil Eye", where he sat for hours beside her hospital bed while she lay in a coma. Then in "Double Exposure", they went for one of their rare nights out, to a restaurant, but when they arrived, there was no proper disabled access. They ended up having to go down the back alley to get in. There was this sweet moment of intimacy as Taggart said: "Blow this. Let's just go home and have a nice takeaway."

'Critics have accused Taggart of being a male chauvinist but I think they misinterpret him. He's old-fashioned and that exasperates Jean. But he treats everyone the same – regardless of their sex. He's just got to be convinced that they can do their job.'

Taggart's first sidekick was Livingstone, who, much to Taggart's irritation, shared a love of the arts with Jean. Their conversations left Taggart out in the cold – he probably thought Gilbert and Sullivan were the full-backs in Celtic's 1954 Cup-winning team. When Neil Duncan, who played Livingstone, decided to leave, Taggart acquired a new sparring partner – fresh-faced, God-fearing, teetotal Mike Jardine, the son of a former colleague. It was not Taggart's idea of blending in with the surroundings to stand at the bar of a tough Glasgow pub and order a pint and an orange juice.

In 1990, a third member of the team made her debut – Jackie Reid. Robert Love says: 'The episode "Death Comes Softly" had a young uniformed community policewoman and we cast an actress named Blythe Duff. She hadn't done television before but I had noticed her once or twice in the theatre and was keen to find a part for her. During the course of making "Death Comes Softly", I thought: "Wait a minute, she's good. This could add a new dimension." It was just a point when I think the series needed something different, so we decided to write her in as a new Detective Constable for "Rogues' Gallery".'

Taggart has certainly fulfilled Robert Love's aim of putting STE on the national map. It is among the country's most-watched programmes with an audience averaging over 12 million. The viewing figures for the 1992 New Year episode 'Violent Delights' reached a staggering 18.3 million. *Taggart* has won a host of awards, including the 1993 Writers' Guild Award for Best Drama Serial and the 1991 BAFTA Scotland Award for Best Drama Series for the episode 'Hostile Witness'. The series has been sold to no fewer than forty-four countries, from Italy to Iceland, Slovenia to Senegal, Algeria to Australia. It was sold to the Eastern Bloc countries even before the Iron Curtain came down.

Taggart is particularly popular in Denmark and France. 'It is dubbed into French,' explains Robert Love, 'and has become a cult show. The French like a hero with flaws and analyse it very seriously. They consider *Taggart* to be part of the film noir genre.'

To what does Robert Love attribute *Taggart's* continuing success? 'It's the classic whodunit. We tell our writers that the trademark of *Taggart* is to keep the viewer guessing right up until the last minute. To sustain a story over three

Despite their frequent conflicts, Taggart and Jean are devoted to one another.

hours we usually include a sub-plot as well, to keep the balls in the air. There is no doubt that Glenn's writing has maintained very high standards over the years, and the other writers we have used – people like Stuart Hepburn and Barry Appleton – have been excellent too. Mark was absolutely the ideal leading man and the supporting cast have been wonderful. I have had tremendous support from people like producer Murray Ferguson and director Alan Macmillan, while the crew have always been totally committed 100 per cent professional. Then there is Glasgow itself. Glasgow is the hidden star of *Taggart*. It looks so good on screen and is different from any other city in the UK. And it holds this incredible fascination for the rest of Britain.'

In addition to French, Taggart's voice has also been dubbed into Chinese and Spanish. Mark McManus remembered one occasion when Taggart's fame in Spain landed him in trouble. 'I was doing a movie out there between *Taggarts*. I have only a halting knowledge of Spanish and used to go to a café where the working men congregated. For weeks, I had been asking for "uno beer".

'One day, I walked in and I immediately thought: "What's wrong?" There was a real atmosphere among these men whom I had got to know. I looked at the telly on the wall and there I was as Taggart, speaking perfect Catalan Spanish! They didn't know it was dubbed – they all thought I'd been winding them up ...'

2
MURDER HE WROTE

Some might say it was poetic justice. There was Glenn Chandler, the man who has dreamed up all manner of ingenious ways of killing people off in *Taggart*, cowering in the corner, fearing for his own life.

He was researching the story 'Nest of Vipers' and, following visits to the Liverpool School of Tropical Medicine and Diseases plus the reptile house at London Zoo, Glenn went out to see a snake collector at High Wycombe in Buckinghamshire.

'Nest of Vipers': Jardine checks this deadly weapon for teeth...

'This chap kept over sixty snakes in his house,' recalls Glenn. 'He had four pythons in the garage alone. The house was seething with snakes, all wandering free except for the venomous ones which he kept in glass tanks. As we chatted, he decided to let two deadly Gaboon vipers out of their tanks in order to feed them with frozen chickens. The snakes immediately stretched their jaws to devour these chickens and everything was fine – until this chap suddenly announced that he was going off to make a phone call.

'"You stay there," he said. "Don't worry. They can't do anything with their mouths full! It will take them twenty minutes to digest those chickens. If they do come towards you, just leg it …"

'I just stood there, scared stiff, watching these extremely venomous snakes just a few feet away, and praying that he would finish his phone call before the twenty minutes was up. Fortunately for me, he did. I was mightily relieved.'

Glenn Chandler's fascination for the macabre has led him to find new and ingenious ways to despatch people in **Taggart**.

Friendly and soft-spoken, Glenn Chandler seems an unlikely person to make murder his business. Nor does his background hint at the macabre pursuits that were to follow.

'All of my family were musical,' he says. 'My grandfather, Frank Moy, was a band leader – he and his orchestra used to play at the Caledonian Hotel in Edinburgh. My father was a member of the band and ended up marrying the band leader's daughter. My mother was an amateur opera singer. They tried to teach me music but I wasn't having any of it. The only thing I could do well at school was write, so I turned to writing instead.'

The irony that an Edinburgh boy should end up making his name writing about Glasgow is not lost on Glenn. 'I was born in Edinburgh, I live in Hertfordshire, which is why I write about Glasgow!' he jokes. 'In fact, in all the time I lived in Edinburgh, I only visited Glasgow once or twice. The first time was to see Ken Russell's film *Women in Love* because Edinburgh Council had banned it. But as a rule, Edinburgh people tend not to go to Glasgow.

'It meant that before I did "Killer", I had to spend three or four days in Glasgow, getting to know the place and the language. It felt like alien territory. I went into pubs just to get the feel of how the locals talk. And not just Taggart but all the names of the characters in "Killer" came from gravestones in Maryhill cemetery.'

Prior to creating *Taggart*, Glenn had moved south to further his ambition of writing for television. 'First, I wrote some fringe theatre plays for places like London's Little Theatre, which is now Stringfellow's night-club. I think it's quite a claim to fame to have had a play put on at Stringfellow's!'

Glenn is justifiably proud of *Taggart* although, with characteristic modesty, he tends to play down the brilliant construction of his scripts. Forty-four and single, he says that some of his ideas come to him when he walks with his black Labrador bitch, Bonnie, in the woods near his Wheathampstead home. 'But mostly my inspiration comes from old murder cases. I've got a large collection of true crime books and often I'll pluck a book off the shelf and read up on an interesting case from yesteryear. You couldn't invent some of the things that actually do happen – they're much more bizarre than fiction. If there's a good case in the news, I'll store it away for possible later use.'

Occasionally, it works the other way round and fact mirrors fiction. Glenn says: 'We did an episode, "Root of Evil", where moneylenders were chopped up with an axe and, at about the time when we were filming, a moneylender

'Murder in Season': Frank Mulholland is injured when John Samson's boat goes up in flames.

really was found chopped up in Glasgow. And shortly after we made "Knife Edge", there was a case in Essex where bits of body turned up at a rubbish depot – just as they had in *Taggart*. Perhaps most worrying was "The Killing Philosophy", which featured a killer nicknamed "The Glasgow Bowman". We showed a group of football supporters chanting, "There's only one Glasgow Bowman" and, sure enough, the following week at Ibrox, Rangers fans started chanting: "There's only one Glasgow Bowman." I thought: "What have I started?"'

The idea for one *Taggart* story originated from Glenn's visit to the Saracen's Head, a famous Glasgow watering hole. 'I was wondering what to write about next when I called in there to see what it was like. I found myself watching two guys in a corner who seemed to be acting most suspiciously. One had a piece of paper in his hand. On the paper, I could see the plan of a house. They talked furtively and whenever anybody came near, the paper was hastily removed from view. I became convinced that they were plotting a murder. So I thought: "That's a good idea. I'll do a story with a publican in it." So I wrote "Murder in Season", where the publican hired a young unemployed guy to bump off his wife.'

Planning each episode takes around two months, during which time Glenn will consult specialists on the chosen subject. 'We're also on good terms with the Strathclyde Police, which means that I can ring them up and ask what a detective would do in a particular set of circumstances.'

One of Glenn Chandler's principal rules when writing *Taggart* is: make sure the murderer has a good motive. 'In her book *Murder and its Motives*, the famous criminologist F. Tennyson Jesse wrote that there were only six motives for murder in the world – gain, revenge, elimination, jealousy, lust and conviction. Sometimes I like to combine them.

'Another rule is that the murderer must always appear in the first episode. We don't suddenly produce the killer out of a hat at the end. You have to give the audience the chance to work it out for themselves. Sometimes I get to the end and think: "This is terribly unfair on the viewer – nobody's ever going to guess this." So I go back and slip in a little clue in an early scene, often in the very first scene when you might still be settling down and making your tea. For example, "Death Call" concerned a woman who was selling surrogate

Not for the squeamish ...

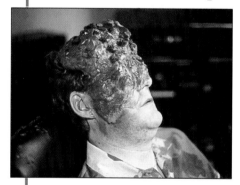

Viewers across the land recoiled in horror at the gruesome spectacle of John Samson, who had seemingly shot himself through the mouth in the *Taggart* story 'Murder in Season', blowing the top of his head clean away. Perhaps they might have emerged from behind the sofa a little sooner had they known that the gaping head wound was largely a combination of mince and chicken bones.

'It's true,' says Fiona Harvey, the make-up designer on *Taggart*, 'and what's more, I put the rest of the chicken in a curry!'

Since *Taggart* has an extraordinarily high mortality rate, Fiona has to keep up the blood count. 'I use proprietary blood. It comes in little pots in different shades and textures. You can buy "Fresh Scab", "Wound-filler Light", "Wound-filler Dark" and so on. I think the trickiest wound had to do in *Taggart* was for "Evil Eye", where a guy had his throat slit and had to be rolled up in a carpet. We use morticians' wax as the base for our wounds but, with the presence of the carpet, that one was a real nightmare to keep on.

'Whenever I need advice about wounds, I go to the forensic department at Glasgow University. They're very helpful. They show you slides of genuine wounds, so there's no way you can afford to be squeamish.'

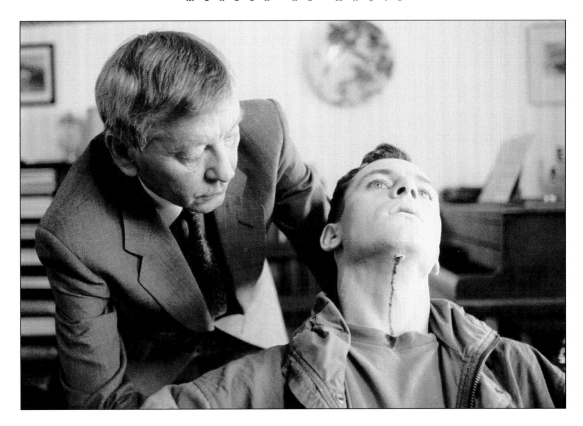

babies and then killing the couples when they arrived with the money. People said to me: "There's no way you could tell that it was about babies. How could you tell that the first two murder victims were going to that woman to collect a surrogate child?" But in the very first shot, the opening titles ended and you saw her walking up the street and she went into a Mothercare shop. Now if you'd spotted that, you would say: "Why was she going into a Mothercare shop when they were going off on holiday together? Why would she be shopping for a baby? She hasn't got a baby." The clue was there.'

John Barr kills property developer Joe Malcolmson (below) before murdering his own twin to evade capture (above).

Glenn has been determined to avoid the stereotypes which beset some detective series. 'There's never been a scene in *Taggart* where they've sat down with a list of suspects and gone through them. I find all that terribly contrived. It's OK in a book but not on television. I also hate detectives with the empty fridge syndrome – where they go home at night to a scruffy flat and an empty fridge and look lonely. Taggart's a three-dimensional character. He's got a wife and a daughter and often his domestic life comes into it.

'In fact, though, I think murderers are probably more interesting than

17

'Nest of Vipers': Jardine and Reid are sent to investigate the theft of some venomous spiders and snakes from a research laboratory.

detectives. I love reading about something from the murderer's point of view. Ruth Rendell is very good because she takes you into the deepest recesses of the criminal mind. Since *Taggart* is essentially a whodunit, it is difficult to see the murderer, but I try to get the best of both worlds. In "Knife Edge", everyone thought the butcher was the murderer because he spent three episodes with the body in the pigeon dookit whereas it turned out that he was just trying to dispose of the body. It was much the same with the old lady in "Gingerbread". It was the next best thing to having the psychology of the murderer.

'In "The Killing Philosophy", which was probably the most violent *Taggart* story, I was able to show two murderers in action because I had the Bowman and the psychopathic philosophy student.

'Taggart says there's no such thing as a clever murderer, which is perfectly true. Most murderers are incredibly inept. Even cops when they try to commit murder make stupid mistakes. Unsolved cases are usually down to luck rather than skill.

'It may sound strange but there is a lot of humour in murder, and I aim to reflect that in *Taggart*. Keith Simpson's account of being a Home Office pathologist contains a wonderful story about him taking the severed head of a girl back to his laboratory for examination. He was just going up to his house at the dead of night when a policeman stopped him, thinking he looked suspicious, and asked Simpson to show him the contents of the box. He reckoned that policeman would never stop anyone again …'

Glenn admits that he has a liking for the macabre. 'I enjoy using things like magpies – I think it comes from living in the country. I find that people enjoy the gruesome angle to *Taggart* – they like bodies being wrapped in blankets and also seeing murders committed. There's nothing more boring than a secondhand corpse! You like to see the knife or whatever going in. Where I can, I tend to avoid gun murders – I find them boring, too.' I think "Nest of Vipers" was my favourite story. The idea for that came about after I'd read a case in which two skeletons were unearthed. I'd always wanted to do something involving venomous snakes so that gave me the opportunity. The thing I enjoyed about it was that the murders took place and yet the murderer was not even on the premises. How do you beat a black mamba in the bed or a

'Gingerbread': Simon Barrow is convinced that his father's brutal murder is connected with the cottage in the woods, but has a hard time convincing Taggart and Jardine.

carpet viper lunging upwards at the speed of a rocket from the doggie food bag? I thought the viper sequence was very well done – it made me jump when I first saw it. And there was the poisonous spider in the pocket at the Burns Supper. That was a quality murder. Very satisfying.'

Taggart is now so well established that Glenn is able to do an off-the-wall story like 'Gingerbread', which was based on the tale of Hansel and Gretel. He also enjoys including moments 'for the *Taggart* buffs'. For example, the only killer to escape Taggart's clutches was James Little in 'Hostile Witness', although he was presumed to have rotted in a container depot. So in 'Gingerbread', there

was a scene with a girl looking at a photograph of Little, and Jardine saying: 'Ah, he's the only one that got away.'

Glenn finds that friends are anxious to become involved in *Taggart* – even if it means meeting a bloody death. 'People come up to me in the pub with suggestions for stories and a friend of mine in Glasgow, Philip Chalmers, said to me once: "I'd love to be a victim in *Taggart*." I said OK. So the first victim in "Gingerbread" was called Philip Chalmers. His name was mentioned every ten minutes. My pal was delighted!'

3
SCENES OF THE CRIME

The city of Glasgow: the 'hidden star' of **Taggart**.

T he City of Glasgow is a film-maker's dream. It is a city of contrasts, boasting some beautifully preserved buildings and more parks and open spaces per acre than any other in Europe, backed by stark high-rise fortresses, which seem to cluster together for safety, and those remaining Victorian tenement blocks which have yet to fall victim to the bulldozer. Few cities in the world combine culture and crime so effectively. Small wonder then that Robert Love calls it the 'hidden star' of *Taggart*.

'It is a very photogenic city,' he says. 'There are plenty of rich settings in and around Glasgow. And it's not just the inner-city areas or smart suburbs such as Bearsden – in no time, you're out in the country with mountains and lochs.

'We decided long ago to avoid the trap which drama from Scotland had fallen into, of looking back to the past – the nostalgia for the great days of shipbuilding. *Taggart* is a series for contemporary Glasgow, showing it warts and all but also showing the good bits. We've got away from the Glasgow of popular myth, the razor gangs.

'*Taggart* is seen as a good advertisement for the city. In fact, the tourist board have approached us about setting out "*Taggart* Trails" in the city. Glaswegians regard it as their own series and Mark McManus as their private property. For example, there was great concern when they read that he was not well.'

Inevitably, some Glaswegians have not always taken kindly to their city being dubbed the murder capital of the world, particularly in 1990 when Glasgow held the title of European City of Culture. 'Some do complain,' admits Robert Love, 'because it doesn't chime with their preferred sanitized view of the city. But we would like to think that we show the city accurately, as it is now. Obviously, the darker side is there because it is a crime series.

'The people of Glasgow are generally very friendly when we go out on location. They are interested in the filming – not like in London, where they

'The Hit Man': The plane crash in this episode was staged at Fenwick Moor in south Glasgow, using elaborate special effects for the explosion (middle).

are a bit blasé about it all. *Taggart* tends to be a passport: when they hear we're filming Taggart, it's a guarantee of co-operation.'

Although *Taggart* has ventured farther afield – to the Scottish Highlands for 'Love Knot' and to the fairy-tale castle of Neuschwanstein in Bavaria for 'Double Jeopardy' (a co-production with the Bavarian Television Service, Bayerischer Rundfunk) –

To stage the actual wreckage, the prop buyers collected bits and pieces of various aircraft. They then matched them up (top) to appear as the debris of Tommy Catto's plane, seen here surrounding Taggart and Jardine (bottom).

most of the filming takes place in Glasgow and its immediate environs. For years, the exterior of Partick Marine Division police station doubled up as Maryhill (*Taggart's* base) but the building was recently renovated, rendering *Taggart* temporarily homeless.

'The old station was just right for us,' says Robert Love. 'It had a nice feel to it. But now Partick have moved to a brand new station and the old building has been done up. We don't want anything too modern for *Taggart*.' Interior scenes of the station are still shot at the old shipyard offices in Whiteinch.

The police officers at Partick used to mingle quite happily with the actors, although Harriet Buchan, who plays Jean Taggart, says there has been the odd

Neil Duncan and Mark McManus on location for 'Death Call'. The Clyde river has always been a prominent feature in **Taggart**.

The production team had to look hard for the right cottage to feature in 'Gingerbread'. What they finally found was a deserted woodman's cottage in the heart of Crieff's woodland, in Stirlingshire.

moment of chaos. 'One time there was a fire alarm when we were filming. When the police arrived, they were terribly mixed up because there were all these pseudo policemen everywhere!

'People often mistake our filming for the real thing. In the story "Hostile Witness", some of the characters were spearheading a campaign for the return of capital punishment. We had a van with a banner draped across it reading: "Bring Back Hanging." Some people thought it was for real and came over and offered to sign a petition.'

Mortuary scenes, of which there are plenty in *Taggart*, are actually filmed at the Glasgow City Mortuary. Robert Robertson, who plays the pathologist Dr Andrews, remembers an eerie coincidence during the filming of the episode "Death Comes Softly". 'We had done a scene in an attic where two girls found a mummified body and then we went to film at the mortuary. But when we arrived, we were held up because there was a real post-mortem in progress ... of a mummified baby. That sent a shiver up my spine.'

When Glenn Chandler first visited the mortuary, he was struck by the matter-of-fact way in which the attendants went about their work – chatting about last night's match while carrying a corpse across the room – and also by a notice on one of the walls. 'It was a masterpiece of understatement. It said something like: "Would

The film crew set up a precarious shot, looking down across the stunning Highlands landscape.

Mark McManus on location in Torridon, surrounded by the beautiful lochs of the Highlands

undertakers coming to collect corpses please make sure that they collect the body which they have requested as this is convenient to all concerned.'"

The Clyde features regularly in *Taggart*. In 'Love Knot' a girl's body is dredged up from the river. Glenn says: 'At first, the script had the dredger operator who brought up the body carving a notch in a piece of wood above his controls and saying to Taggart: "This is my eighth body." But when we checked it out, we found it was more likely to be his eightieth body. Any eighth body was likely to be the eighth that week. They get all sorts – jumpers, murder victims, car accidents, drunks who fall in, you name it. Apparently, they once pulled out three in a single day!'

Taggart may be one of Glasgow's favourite sons but not everyone welcomes the production team with open arms, Robert Love confesses: 'British Rail haven't spoken to us since "Ring of Deceit". They won't let us film at stations now because in that story, we implied that people could get mugged at unattended stations – which is perfectly true – and also because the murderer was a British Rail employer …'

4
TAGGART PROFILE

If ever a man's popularity was summed up by his funeral, that man was Mark McManus. When he died in June 1994 at the age of fifty-nine, nearly 2,000 Glaswegians took to the street to pay their respects. Many had never even met the man, others were little more than nodding acquaintances, but all spoke of losing a friend. That sentiment was echoed by the Strathclyde police. They turned out in force to say farewell to the actor who had done so much good work for them, both in the guise of Jim Taggart and off screen.

Three months before Mark's death, I had the pleasure of interviewing him at the Scottish Television studios. We chatted about his colourful life, one which in the latter days was clouded with sadness.

Mark McManus never forgot his introduction to the role of Taggart. It was an experience which would have turned the stomach of even the hard-boiled detective. Mark explained: 'A close friend of mine was a detective in Glasgow's "A" Division. I'd just landed the part of Taggart and I didn't know much about detective work. So he said: "Would you like me to arrange for you to do a couple of night shifts with the boys?"

'Anyway, I went along for the ride and after dealing with the usual couple of fracas, they were called to a block of flats where a woman hadn't been seen for a few days. The two cops I was with went up to the flat, but then one came back and said: "Mark, I think you'd better sit in the motor. You're not gonna like this."

Mark McManus as the granite-faced detective, Chief Inspector Jim Taggart.

'They'd found the woman's body. She'd been lying dead in her flat for four days. Her three cats had just started to eat her. …Thank God I never saw any of it. But at the end of the shift, they called it a quiet night. I thought, if this is a quiet night, I hate to think what a busy one's like!'

Detective Chief Inspector Jim Taggart is a popular figure with Strathclyde Police. 'Aye, we get a good reaction from them,' said Mark. 'One of the strengths of *Taggart* is that we've tried to keep it realistic. Actual detective work is very tiring. They work long hours and spend half their time on paperwork.

'Flesh and Blood': Taggart and Jardine pick their way through the rubble of George McKnight's country cottage after it is devastated by an explosion.

We've managed to show that. No wonder they get annoyed when some thug comes up before the Sheriff and gets 120 hours' community service. They've worked months on that case and he's got away with it.'

He himself bore the scars from a brutal mugging in 1990. 'I was on West Nile Street in the city centre, on my way home from work. I never saw the guy – he just came at me fast. Bash. I thought: "Jesus Christ, what's that?" Then I saw he had a blade. He got me to the ground and ran off.

'The one witness came over, lifted me up and said: "I think we'd better take you to hospital, Mark, because blood's pouring out of your arm."

'I said: "Wait a minute, I've got £80 in my back pocket." And it was still there. He hadn't dipped me. I could've understood it almost if I'd been robbed, but it was done out of malice. Can you believe that?'

In spite of the attack, Mark still had a love affair with his native city. 'I'm not a nationalist but I love Glasgow dearly, so I'm proud of *Taggart*. I know Glasgow and its people and I've tried to evoke what the city can be like – sometimes good, sometimes bad, like all big cities. I've been all over the world, to Australia, Canada, America, you name it, but this dear green city is the place I call home.'

The people certainly took Mark to their hearts. 'When we're out filming,' he said, 'they come up to me and want to shake me by the hand. It's good to have your work appreciated.'

Mark McManus was born the son of a miner in the Lanarkshire town of Hamilton, just outside Glasgow. In those days, it was naturally assumed by most parents that the mining tradition would be carried on by their offspring, but Mark's father did not adhere to this belief and desperately wanted something better for his son. 'We had no money,' recalled Mark, 'but then neither did anyone else in the community.'

As a boy, he took up boxing and boosted his pocket money by picking vegetables, but the reality of unemployment hit home when he left school. With few qualifications, he was faced with two possibilities – the dole or the pit. He chose the latter, but quickly became disenchanted and opted instead for a job as a timber porter at Govan docks.

By the age of twenty-two, he had grown restless and decided to seek fame and fortune elsewhere. With dreams of wealth, he set off for Australia in the finest pioneering spirit. Unfortunately, Australia was going through a depression and work was scarce. After a brief period wandering from town to town, he settled in Sydney.

'I lived in a crummy boarding house, run by a stingy Scots landlady whose idea of breakfast every morning was a cup of tea and one frankfurter. There were lots of young lads there – Greeks, Poles, Danes, Italians – and as I spoke her language, I was elected to go and complain. She promised to improve things. And she did – from then on, we got a cup of tea, one frankfurter and a dod of tomato sauce!'

Mark got a job at Sydney docks, labouring in temperatures of up to 110 degrees and supplementing his income with a spot of part-time boxing. 'The dockyards didn't pay that much so I would fight on Friday and Saturday nights for the extra cash. Boxing was easy money, mainly because I enjoyed it.'

He reckoned he collected seventy-two stitches in twenty-five bouts, the majority acquired in his final fight, when he lost his unbeaten tag to 'a local aborigine giant. My face was rearranged and my nose reshaped during that fight. After that, I decided enough was enough.'

The dockers' union had its own amateur theatre group, so Mark joined up and soon got his Equity card. He accepted an offer to join a small touring company and embarked on a 38,000-mile tour of the Australian outback, performing potted Shakespeare to audiences in remote bush towns. His first professional role was in *Macbeth* – as a witch! Television parts came next, taking him to such exotic locations as Tahiti, Fiji, New Guinea and the Solomon Islands, and including a stint alongside the greatest Australian television star of all, Skippy the bush kangaroo.

Mark's willingness to take risks earned him the Tommy Steele role as the song-and-dance man in an Australian production of the musical *Half a Sixpence*. 'I was asked if I could sing and dance. I said: "No, but I could learn." So I spent two months taking tap-dance lessons in Sydney.'

Half a Sixpence took Mark to America, but it was in Australia that his big break came when director Tony Richardson offered him a part alongside Mick Jagger in the 1970 film *Ned Kelly*. 'I can't speak highly enough of Mickey,' said Mark. 'He's a great guy – nice, easy-going, down-to-earth. Any time we hit the cities, though, it was horrendous. Girls were tearing him to bits, ripping his clothes, pulling out his hair by the handful. I don't know how he coped.'

Mick Jagger wasn't the only one to make a good impression. Tony Richardson was so taken by Mark's work on the film that he advised him to return to Britain to further his acting career. Mark ended his exile in 1971 and settled in London with his first wife and his two children, Christopher and Kate. A spell at the Royal Court Theatre was followed by one at the National, during which time he appeared with the likes of Sir John Gielgud and Sir Ralph Richardson. It was a far cry from Sydney docks.

But it was in television that Mark made his name in the 1970s – in series such as *The Brothers*, *Colditz*, *The Foundation*, *Strangers* and the title role in *Sam*, a highly successful drama series set in the 1930s about a miner tired of his lot who decided to fight his way out of the pits. It could have been based on Mark McManus's own life story …

And so to *Taggart*. 'He is a man of the people and so am I,' said Mark. 'He's rude and horrible but he has a cocky charm. Like him, I'm really a street guy at heart. It's where I'm happiest. I've worked in some dreadful places in my life so I know I'm really lucky to have this job. I never pass a factory without thinking about those days and how lucky I have been.'

He knew that *Taggart* has a winning formula. 'Viewers love a whodunit. I personally like the three-parters and I think they do too. There is a break of a week and it leaves a carrot dangling for the viewer. It's a good format. It also has to be said that the series is well written and looks good on screen.'

Mark had strict views about *Taggart*. 'When I agreed to do it, I said that

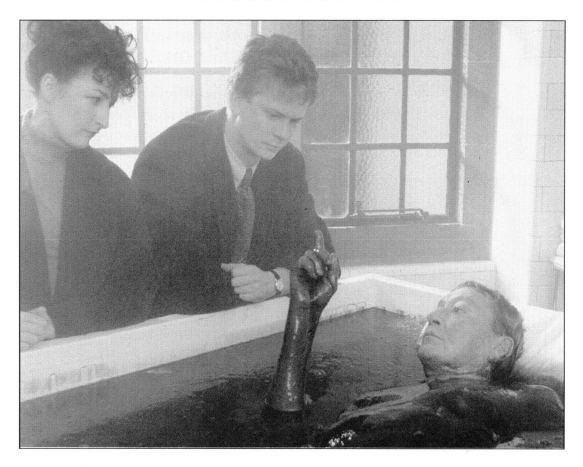

there should be no anglicized accents, no compromises on dialects. I refused to use the word "police". It has to be "polis".

'I didn't want any smoking on *Taggart* either. One day on the London Underground a twelve-year-old boy came up to me and said: "Hey, I saw you in *Bulman* last night. I love the way you hold your fag. Dead cool." I was horrified kids might think I was encouraging them to smoke, so I insisted on the no-smoking rule on *Taggart*.

'I also dug in my heels about not doing any bedroom scenes. Although Taggart has marital problems from time to time and is attracted by other women, I believe that the viewer should never see him under the sheets with another woman.'

Mark joked that, just occasionally, the burden of playing such an accomplished detective as Taggart could be too heavy. 'I'm expected to know everything! I remember once I was in a trendy city-centre pub with lots of subdued lighting and dark corridors. I made my way to the toilets but when I opened the door, a woman looked up at me in a state of shock. Before I could mumble my apologies, she bawled: "Supposed to be a detective and ye canny

'Fatal Inheritance': When Reid and Jardine investigate Janet Napier's health farm, the last thing they expect to be greeted with is the sight of Taggart up to his ears in it.

even find the Gents …"' Taggart would have given him a roasting too.

Mark may have considered that he had been lucky in work, but, off-screen, he endured more than his fair share of heartache in the last years of his life. Within the space of two years, he lost his mother, both sisters (at tragically young ages), and then, in October 1993, his second wife, Marion, following a brave battle against cancer. Mark had met Marion, a former costume designer with Scottish Television, on the set of *Taggart* and they had married in 1986.

'Funeral Rites': Is Jean's friend, Maggie Davidson, the helpless invalid she appears to be? Taggart aims to find out.

So many fans turned up for the wedding that the police had to cordon off the street.

'Aye, it's been a terrible couple of years,' Mark reflected. 'I was devastated when we first learned about Marion's illness. But I've always been a fighter. Unless you're brave, you're nothing. That's why I've thrown myself into my work. You have to be a soldier. Marion wouldn't have wanted me to suddenly drop my bundle.'

Happily, Mark had no shortage of friends. Among them was James Macpherson, who plays Jardine. It was one of the proudest moments of Mark's life when James asked him to be godfather to his daughter Katie. 'It was a great honour,' said Mark. 'For me, one of the most gratifying aspects of working on *Taggart* has been to see first Neil Duncan and then James come in as raw boys and to watch them develop as fine actors.'

Any breaks in filming were usually taken up with Mark's passion for breeding butterflies, a throwback to his childhood when he spent hours watching butterflies and birds on the banks of the Clyde. 'I love every minute of it,' he enthused. 'It's my way of putting something back into the world. I feel that a lot of damage has been done to Britain with pesticides. When I was a boy, I used to see butterflies everywhere. Now you don't see many. So by breeding them and releasing them into the wild, I hope to increase the numbers. I used to breed canaries and finches, but the butterflies seemed to take over. I suppose the canaries were a hangover from the family days as miners. I've always loved horses too. When I was a boy, I used to spend my holidays on a farm, lifting hay. The groom there asked me if I wanted to work with him and so my passion for Clydesdale horses started. Now I breed them – I suppose I can't make up my mind whether I'm an actor or a farmer!'

Sadly, he never had the chance to find out.

5

COLLEAGUES AND NEXT OF KIN

Detective Inspector Mike Jardine

One person who is never likely to be put off by the sight of a corpse in *Taggart* is James Macpherson, who plays Mike Jardine. For James spent five years as a laboratory technician at Glasgow's Institute of Neurological Studies.

'It was my job to go down to the morgue every Monday to collect the brains for pickling! So in *Taggart*, when we film at the Glasgow City Mortuary, I'm usually the one sent in to see if it's all clear because, in my old job, I'd seen it all before. It was no problem. Mind you, when we did the story where Jardine had to faint at the sight of a corpse, I had very bad gastro-enteritis. On that occasion, there really was no acting required.'

Detective Sergeant Mike Jardine: 'out of the same drawer' as Taggart.

Like Mark McManus, James was raised in Hamilton. He left Hamilton Grammar School at seventeen to work in the lab (where he met his future wife, Jacqui) and then decided to go for an interview as a policeman. 'But I realized at the first interview that I'm not hard enough for the job. I'm basically a softie. It just wasn't me. I didn't have that special confidence which officers need every day. People say you need confidence to go on stage or before the camera, but if I duff my lines, I can do them again. A bobby only has one chance to get it right.'

Having concluded that he was not cut out for a life in the force, James's thoughts turned to acting. He joined an amateur dramatics group in Motherwell before moving on to East Kilbride repertory theatre and a place in drama school. 'The first day at drama school, everyone had to speak about themselves and why they wanted to act. All the others were saying they'd wanted to be an actor since they were a foetus, and when my turn came, I said: "Since last month."'

'The Hit Man':
Jardine discovers
the body of Billy
Boyce.

After landing the part of Hugh Hamilton in Radio Four's *Citizens*, his television career began to take off. 'While I was based in London, I came up to Scotland to audition for director Hal Duncan, for a children's series called *Dramarama*. I didn't get that part and returned to London. Then in 1986, Hal told my agent that the part of Jardine was coming up in *Taggart* and that he wanted to see me again. I was puzzled because he already knew me. He said afterwards that he'd just wanted to see if I'd got my Glasgow accent back. Being in London, I'd tightened my accent because I was fed up with having to repeat myself. But within two weeks of returning to Glasgow, I'd got it back.

'Jardine originally came in as a foil to Livingstone, but then Neil Duncan, who played Livingstone, left after my first story. I thought they'd bring in someone else, and it was a case of everybody knowing I was going to be the new sidekick except me.

'I was really green at first,' cringes James. 'I knew nothing about the technical side of filming. For instance, when the crew are shooting, they shout "mark" and bang the clapperboard. Every time they shouted "mark", I looked at Mark McManus, who was sitting there calmly reading his book, not taking a blind bit of notice of them. I couldn't understand why he didn't jump up when they shouted his name!'

Jardine was equally raw in the early days. The son of an old police sergeant colleague of Taggart who had died of alcoholism, he had known Taggart for years. Indeed, Taggart used to bounce young Mike on his knee. 'Taggart always liked Jardine,' says James, 'because "they came out of the same drawer", as he put it. But there had to be something to create conflict between the two, so they introduced the Christian bit and the non-drinking. Initially, Jardine reacted to Taggart's jibes by putting his head down; next, he'd laugh; and now he argues back and there's no laugh at the end. The character has evolved – Jardine has become more confident.

'Little old ladies used to stop me in the street and say, "Poor boy", in reaction to the way Taggart treated me, but there's not so much of that now.'

Jardine's rapid rise through the ranks has provoked much amusement from James Macpherson's Uncle Iain, a real Glasgow Chief Inspector. James says: 'I started as a Detective Constable and quickly became a Detective Sergeant. Uncle Iain said it took him twenty years to do that! When he was made up to Chief Inspector, I got a framed photo of Mark and got Mark to sign it: "From one Chief Inspector to another." I went to deliver it to my uncle's house one day. Nobody was home so I broke in through the window he'd left open. When he returned, I gave him a lecture about crime prevention …'

At thirty-four, James is the proud father of Jamie, 6, Katie, 3, and Jack, 1. Not that you'd know it from some of the things he gets called in the street. 'I remember once I was walking along the road and a crowd of workmen shouted: "Eh, Jardine!" I beamed with pride and turned round. Then one of them shouted: "You're a poof!" That's the kind of place Glasgow is. I love it.'

James was very close to Mark McManus. 'I remember the first words he ever spoke to me. He said: "It's a bugger of a first day, Jim," and, as usual, he was right. There I was, half past seven in the morning, up to my knees in mud – it was freezing cold, rain was pouring down – stuck out in a field. And from then on, I knew we would be friends. I had eight years with the man, and every day I knew I'd go into work and that he'd make me laugh. I miss him.'

James is a big fan of Glenn Chandler's scripts. 'The amazing thing is that so many are based on real cases. Take "Forbidden Fruit", with the guy at the clinic. Glenn said he had to tone it down to only sixty women impregnated by the doctor. Apparently, it really happened in the USA, but with 120 women. That was great because I knew people would say: "Ach, that would never happen." So the next day in the supermarket, I had my armoury.

'The great thing about Glenn's scripts is you never tire of them – you always want to read them right the way through. I remember once my wife, my eldest son and I were with Mark and his late wife, Marion, at their cottage. The repeats of *Taggart* were on and Mark said: "D'ye want to come and watch it? We'll have an ego trip." So we all sat down and watched it. About three-quarters of the way through, Mark turned to me and said: "James, I remember who did it, but for the life of me, I can't remember why!"'

Detective Sergeant Jackie Reid

Blythe Duff's heart sank when she read in the script that Jackie Reid was to be confronted in an attic by a bat.

'Because British bats are quite small, they wanted a big fruit bat so that it would register on screen. I said: "If you don't mind, I'd rather have somebody on set to handle the bat." I just didn't fancy it at all. Anyway, the day before we were due to do it, the bat handler was bitten by a monkey so we used a pigeon instead!

'Glenn Chandler's got this thing about animals,' says Blythe. 'He likes to include magpies, snakes and bats. For "Nest of Vipers", I had to have a ratsnake round my neck. The snake handler came along to the readthrough, so we all had a chance to hold the snakes before filming. The funny thing was, he brought them in an ordinary sports bag. You could imagine him sitting with the bag on the bus …'

Detective Constable Jackie Reid: she has gradually proved herself tough enough live up to Taggart's expectations.

Blythe had wanted to be an actress ever since the day she played second witch in a school production of *The Wizard of Oz*. The only other ambition she can recall was a brief desire to be a mounted policewoman, but in the end, acting prevailed. She spent seven years doing theatre work before making her television debut in *Taggart*.

Blythe had a pleasant surprise on her first day filming *Taggart*. 'I had worked briefly with the Scottish Opera Chorus the previous year, so I was amazed when I turned up for my first day to find all my old friends waiting for me. They were playing the part of a festival chorus and, by pure coincidence, happened to be on set the same day as me.'

'After that supporting role as a community policewoman in "Death Comes Softly", it was decided to promote me in "Rogues' Gallery" by seconding me to the CID. The producers explained that I'd be driving Taggart and his assistant around. They'd assumed I had a driving licence, but I hadn't. I couldn't drive. Filming was just three weeks away so I took a crash course – not literally – of lessons. But when I sat my test, I failed. I was absolutely devastated. When the director phoned me the next day, I was so shattered I could barely speak to him. I had to wait another twenty-eight days for a second test, and we were well into filming by then. I had this vision of having to drive Taggart around in L-plates! Luckily, I passed my test the second time – just in time to film the main driving scenes – although, ironically, the day after passing, I was being filmed on a tow-rope.

'I like the way Reid has been eased into the programme,' adds Blythe. 'I think there was a need for a woman in the series. I also like her as a character –

she's got a sense of humour, she works hard and she's good at her job.'

Blythe, who is thirty-one, single and lives in Glasgow, is only too aware that the world of television is not one of pure unadulterated glamour. 'I remember on "Nest of Vipers" we did a night shoot on the Stepps bypass, which was then under construction. It had been pouring with rain for hours, turning the place into a quagmire. We were all issued with wellies but the mud was so deep that we just kept sinking right in. It became virtually impossible even to lift your feet. The final straw came when one of the crew members became completely trapped. Someone had to get another pair of wellies, then lift him out of the pair he was in, which were left submerged and firmly stuck.

'There is so much rain in Glasgow that we dread filming a script which says "nights with rain". Unfortunately, Taggart and Jardine can look very cool with their hair wet, but Jackie Reid looks like a drowned rat.'

Like everyone else on the series, Blythe was deeply saddened by the death of Mark McManus. 'He was probably one of the most generous stars you'll ever find. Obviously, as the new girl, I was bit apprehensive at first, but he made it very easy for you to fit in.

Blythe's success in *Taggart* is a far cry from the two years she spent as a YOP actress, doing community theatre all over Glasgow for £25 a week. 'At a community hall in Maryhill, we were preparing to do Under Milk Wood when I heard this thud while we were backstage. Someone in the audience had thrown darts at the set. I said: "I just want to see there's three darts going in or I'm going nowhere …"'

Superintendent Jack McVitie

As the hard-nosed Jack McVitie, Iain Anders is the scourge of Glasgow's criminal classes, but in his off-screen role as a legal managing clerk, it is the police who sometimes feel the rough edge of his tongue.

'I used to work for a firm of solicitors,' says sixty-one-year-old Iain, 'but for the last five years, I have had my own firm in London. My legal work means I spend a lot of my time in police stations, making a nuisance of myself. The police are trying to get some presumed villain to talk and I seek to prevent this. I'm afraid the police have to put up with me – that's what I'm there for. Most of my clients think it's a great laugh that I play a copper on television.

'It means that my two roles in life are complete opposites. It's a nice irony. And it's not too difficult to combine them both. I've got an assistant, so I manage to fit my legal work in between acting. One of the nice things about having a day job is that I can turn down parts. I don't have to do something if I don't want to.'

Iain, who also finds time to teach bridge, has often veered from one side of the law to the other in his acting career. 'My first paid job was carrying a spear at Birmingham Rep, in a production of *Henry V* starring Albert Finney. I got

Superintendent Jack McVitie: 'The Biscuit'. He and Taggart have little in common but they maintain a healthy mutual respect.

£3 a week for that. But there was a time when I used to play policemen and villains alternately every year in *Z Cars* and *Softly, Softly*.' Iain, who later appeared in *The Gentle Touch*, *Shoestring* and *Juliet Bravo*, says the highest rank he ever achieved was Chief Superintendent in *Softly, Softly*.

'Of course I've done other things as well. I particularly enjoyed appearing in two R.F. Delderfield serials – *A Horseman Riding By* and *Diana*. They were character parts, requiring me to age from forty to seventy-something.'

Iain is a big fan of Glenn Chandler's inventive plots for *Taggart*. And he is as eager as everyone else to find out who the killer is. 'Whenever I first read the *Taggart* script, I don't tell anyone who the murderer is – not even my wife. She also likes to read the scripts, but she won't read the end because it would spoil it for her.'

So what does Iain think of 'The Biscuit'? 'McVitie is pompous, bureaucratic, but not without humour and not unsympathetic to his subordinates, although sometimes he gives that impression. He also has a difficult and childless domestic life.'

And thereby hangs a tale, for Iain confesses that Jack McVitie, pillar of the community, has a dark secret. 'It has to be told,' laughs Iain. 'McVitie has had three different wives! The actress who usually plays Mrs McVitie is Mona Bruce, but if it's only a very small part, they use an extra. That's happened twice. I'm not sure what they'd make of it at force headquarters …'

Jean Taggart

Meeting actress Harriet Buchan for the first time comes as a great shock to many people – they are amazed that she can walk.

'A lot of people expect to see me in a wheelchair,' says Harriet, who plays Taggart's paralysed wife Jean, 'including, and I take that as a compliment, those that are in a wheelchair themselves.'

To research the part, Harriet met Betty Wilson, a Glasgow woman who has had to use a wheelchair for over twenty years. 'Like Jean Taggart, Betty is paralysed from the waist down,' says Harriet. 'Betty advised me on how I should look in a wheelchair – she said you look round-shouldered. Even when

I sit in an ordinary chair now, I sometimes find myself behaving as if I'm in a wheelchair. The other thing is, when I sit in a wheelchair, I immediately feel all the blood rushing from my waist down as if I can't feel anything. It's as if I really am paralysed. It's strange.

Playing Jean has greatly increased Harriet's awareness of the problems facing wheelchair-users. 'I now go round looking for ramps, and every time I pop into a shop, I realize that my screen character would find it virtually impossible.

'The lovely thing about Jean is that she's such a positive person. She seems to inspire others. One of my most cherished moments was being stopped by a woman in Sauchiehall Street. She had been a nurse but had given up her job to look after her husband, who was virtually confined to a wheelchair because he suffered from a heart condition. He had been ready to give up on life, but she told me that it was because Jean had gone off to Canada on her own that they too went to Canada. He had never been on holiday before, but because Jean had managed it, he'd decided to give it a go. It turned their lives around.'

Glasgow-born Harriet trained at the Royal Academy of Music in London. She began work as a music teacher until an attack of acute laryngitis left her without a voice for a number of months. Turning to acting, she went on to appear in series such as *Garnock Way* and *Sutherland's Law*, and had her hair sprayed orange to play a witch in a BBC schools programme.

In 1981, a serious illness threatened to end her acting career. Harriet was diagnosed as having cancer of the left vocal cord. 'It took a year of radiotherapy before I recovered. *Taggart* was my first job afterwards and I suppose, in an odd way, my illness may have helped me to get the part because people who have had chronic illnesses, like myself and Jean, do have a certain look. It's different from that of a hale and hearty person.'

Jean Taggart: She finds Taggart exasperating at times but has no problem in telling him what she thinks of him.

Harriet also runs her own voice workshops. 'I do psychophysical voice work, with tuition in song and harmonic chant. I offer it as a form of therapy for people with disabilities not dissimilar to Jean Taggart. I have even taken my workshops to prisons. It's my belief that everybody should be singing. It tunes the whole body and mind. You cannot sing and be sad.'

One voice you might expect Harriet to have heard enough of is that of Taggart himself. Yet she defends him stoutly. 'People love Taggart as a person, you know, so that whilst some say to me, "Why do you let that old so-and-so treat you like that?", others say, "Will you not stop nagging that poor man!"'

Dr Stephen Andrews

Short of vultures hovering over Sauchiehall Street, Glaswegians have come to acknowledge that the surest sign that foul play has been committed in their city is the sight of actor Robert Robertson.

Robert, who plays police pathologist Dr Andrews, recalls an incident in the early days of *Taggart*. 'I was walking up to the Scottish Television headquarters when one of the cleaners called over to me: "Oh Christ, another murder!" Taken aback, I said: "What, where?" He said: "No, you. Whenever I see you, I know there's going to be another murder!"

'It's perfectly true of course,' laughs Robert. 'We've killed off something like ninety victims in *Taggart* so far. With all these murders, it would make Glasgow worse than Chicago at the time of Al Capone!'

Born in the home of golf, St Andrews, Robert's decision to take up acting led him to weekly rep in Aylesbury in 1948, where the assistant stage manager was a young Ronnie Barker. 'But acting was not considered a proper job in those days,' laments Robert, 'so I went into business. For twelve years, between 1953 and 1965, I was sales director of a brick company in Solihull – we specialized in hand-made bricks. Even so, I kept my hand in with a little theatre company.'

Dr Stephen Andrews: the aimiable police pathologist is a vital source of help for Taggart.

He continued to dabble mainly in theatre work until he landed the part of Dr Andrews – thanks to a plea to his agent. Robert says: 'For six years before "Killer", I'd been devoting my life almost exclusively to getting a theatre built in Dundee where I live. We achieved it in 1982 and I thought, now this is done, if I'm not careful, I could be the forgotten man of the business. So I said to my agent, who I hadn't really bothered for years: "You'd better start putting me about." A few weeks later, my agent called me and said: "Could you get across to Glasgow to see director Laurence Moody, who's casting 'Killer'?"

'I did, and Laurence thought I might fit in, but was honest enough to confess: "There's absolutely no money." I said: "It doesn't matter – I just want to get my face seen again."'

Robert has been a fixture ever since, although he did miss "Forbidden Fruit" after suffering a heart attack in August 1993. 'It just means I no longer do star jumps first thing in the morning!'

Robert is the first to admit that his knowledge of forensics is minimal. 'I just play the script and rely to a large extent on the writers getting their facts right. Inevitably I've picked up little things along the way but, in truth, I could no more do the job of pathologist than climb Mount Everest.'

Detective Sergeant Peter Livingstone

Neil Duncan was tailor-made for the role of Taggart's first right-hand man, Peter Livingstone. 'Like Livingstone, I was born in Edinburgh, I came from a respectable middle-class family and I had a university background. My father was a Professor of Scottish History at Glasgow University and I studied physics for a year at Dundee University. So I had quite a bit in common with the man who was to become my alter ego.

'Added to which, although there were no police connections in my family, I did once arrest a drunk driver while I was at drama school. And I spent a year working as a technician with a vet in Glasgow, cutting up dead dogs and the like. It was all good training for dealing with the corpses in *Taggart*.'

Neil was appearing in his first major television production, a Scottish Television play entitled *Out in the Open*, with Roy Marsden, when he was advised to have a word with Laurence Moody, the director of 'Killer'. 'I had a brief conversation with Laurence,' remembers Neil. 'I tried to sound intelligent, and three days later I was offered the role of Livingstone. In many respects, my relationship with Mark McManus was the same as Livingstone's with Taggart – Livingstone and I were both new recruits, starting out.

'After doing "Killer" and five more *Taggart*s, I decided I wanted to move on to other things – I didn't want to be typecast. It was a hard decision to make. I didn't want to leave my friends on the series but I knew that *Taggart* would continue because he was the central character.'

Although he still has a flat in London, Neil now spends part of the year in Los Angeles. 'When I first went to the States, I thought: "Who'd want to employ a six foot three Scottish actor in Los Angeles?" But I've cornered the market – I'm the only six foot three Scottish actor in Los Angeles!

'Things are working out well, and I was delighted to get the call to come back and do the *Taggart* story "Forbidden Fruit" last year. It coincided with work on a four-hour mini-series for NBC called *Dazzle*, in which I play a sleazy tabloid newspaper owner, so I found myself commuting across the Atlantic like a jet-setter.'

Neil remains full of admiration for *Taggart*. 'They are good, honest, down-to-earth thrillers in which even the minor characters are so well drawn. Mind you, sometimes it was all over and I still didn't know who'd done it!'

Detective Sergeant Peter Livingstone: Taggart's first side-kick was one of the new breed of graduate policeman. He and Taggart experienced an uneasy relationship at first.

6

THE MARYHILL FILES

KNIFE EDGE

Transmission dates:
24 February
–10 March 1986
Writer: Glenn Chandler
Producer: Robert Love
Director: Haldane Duncan

SUPPORTING CAST:
DET. SGT. KENNY FORFAR
– Stuart Hepburn
FRED SWAN
– Andrew McCulloch
GEORGE BRYCE
– Alex Norton
ALEX DEWAR
– Christian Rodska
SCOTT ADAIR
– Iain Glen
JUDY MORRIS
– Siobhan Redmond
ROSY FRENCH
– Corinne Harris
BETTY SWAN
– Jan Wilson
RHONA CAMERON
– Claire Nielson
ANGUS ROBINSON
– Finlay Welsh
DAVE MCSWEAN
– Dave Anderson
EDNA BRYCE
– Monica Brady
JANE FORFAR
– Judy Sweeney
ZACH STEVENS
– Martin Black
CAROLINE PATON
– Julie Miller
MRS BARNET
– Nancy Mitchell

The phone rang in Taggart's office. The information imparted by the caller immediately brightened his morning.

'Get your skates on Peter,' he called to Livingstone. 'We've got a severed leg near the Erskine Bridge.'

'Human?'

'Naw,' replied Taggart, wondering whether you needed a university education to ask such stupid questions. 'The kind you put mint sauce on!'

In the shadow of the Erskine Bridge, they learned that a van driver had pulled into a layby on a dual carriageway at eight-thirty that morning, and descended a grassy bank with the intention of emptying his bladder. Doing up his zip, he had suddenly spotted an object about two-and-a-half feet long wrapped in a piece of tartan rug and tied with string, lying among a pile of rubbish. Curious, he had gone over for a closer look and, to his horror, had seen that through an open end was protruding a stockinged human foot.

It seemed likely that the limb had been thrown from a car. McVitie was anxious for the case to be solved within a fortnight, since he was then off to Bali for three weeks with his wife, but the only lead at that stage came when house-to-house enquiries produced a woman who had seen a gang of Hell's Angels parked near the layby three days earlier.

Taggart was less than enthusiastic. 'Hell's Angels, that's all we need!'

The following morning saw a more significant development. Sitting peacefully on a riverbank, a fisherman reeled in an object wrapped in a piece of tartan rug. It was the other leg.

'That'll make a shapely pair, Jim,' said Dr Andrews, peeling away the folds of the sodden rug. 'Hasn't been in the water long. I'd say about a day or two. From the state of decomposition of the other leg, you're looking for a woman who was killed about six days ago.'

'Which means he's in no hurry to get rid of the pieces,' deduced Taggart, knowing full well that a cool killer is always more difficult to apprehend than

one who panics. Taggart had come to rely on Andrews providing instant answers, but here he was of little help.

'Impossible, of course, to tell you how she was killed,' said the pathologist, almost apologetically, 'until we get the rest of her.'

'Would you like to narrow that age down at all?' asked Taggart, hopefully.

'Thirty-five-ish. That's a big ish.'

'Toes seem buckled together.'

'Yes. From wearing ill-fitting shoes. Majority of women do.'

Taggart allowed his exasperation to get the better of him. 'I don't suppose you've spotted something useful. Like a name tattooed on the thigh?'

As news of the find spread, a man named Angus Robinson informed Taggart that he had reported his wife missing ten days earlier. They had been married seventeen years and there appeared to be no obvious reason why she should have left her husband and four children.

Livingstone was glad to be out of the office, away from the rough edge of Taggart's tongue. Besides, it was a beautiful morning, just right for pursuing a line of enquiry out in the country. As he was heading back towards Maryhill, the sunshine streaming through the windscreen, he glanced in his rear-view

Whose leg is it, anyway?

Much to
Livingstone's relief,
Taggart turns
up when the younger
detective finds
himself surrounded
by a gang of
Hell's Angels.

mirror and realized that he was being followed by a gang of Hell's Angels. He tried hard to be rational. Maybe they just wanted to pass. So he slowed down, giving them the opportunity to overtake, hoping to God that all he would see in seconds was a cloud of dust and exhaust fumes. Instead, they closed in menacingly on both sides, hooting in harmony. Livingstone felt distinctly intimidated. He sounded his horn. It was a hopeless gesture. More extreme measures were needed – he radioed for urgent assistance.

To Livingstone's immeasurable relief, the bikers took the hint and roared off. He followed them at a discreet distance and saw a straggler turn off the road towards a disused stables. Knowing that back-up was on its way, he decided to investigate. Perhaps there was some minor charge he could haul them in on in return for giving him such a fright.

The stables seemed deserted. Gingerly, he stepped out of the car. Suddenly the air was pierced by the sound of a girl's scream. Then another. Casting caution to the wind, he rushed into the building and immediately found himself surrounded. The girl he had heard looked anything but distressed.

'Police,' announced Livingstone, flourishing his ID card in the hope that it would ensure him a safe passage.

The gang leader, Zach Stevens, silently took the card, bit it in half and dropped it into a pile of horse manure.

'Well, I never did like it much anyway,' stammered Livingstone. He tried another tactic. 'I used to have a bike – not quite as big as those down there.'

The approaching sirens did nothing to deter the Angels. Another chapter member produced a chain from his back pocket.

Livingstone feared the worst. 'I wouldn't, if I were you.'

Suddenly seized by two others, Livingstone was powerless as the Angel looped the chain around his neck and forced him into a kiss.

Taggart's arrival produced a different response. The Angel spat. Taggart turned calmly. 'The last person who did that near me wore his balls home as earrings.'

He hauled Stevens in for questioning. The leader of the pack let it be known that he was not in the habit of helping the police. It was bad for his image. Eventually he admitted to seeing a car pull up and somebody throw an object down the bank, but he was unable to describe either the occupant or the car. 'I'm a biker, I don't look at cars.'

Concerned friends and relatives continued to come forward with stories of missing persons. One absentee was Mrs Betty Swan, reported missing by a neighbour, Mrs Barnet. However, as Taggart and Livingstone began to break into the Swan house, Mrs Swan arrived home. She was not amused.

'What the hell are you doing?' she demanded, seeing Mrs Barnet walking up her path.

'We thought you were dead,' answered her neighbour. 'I wasn't to know, was I?'

'Dead?' repeated an incredulous Betty Swan.

'Well, nobody's seen you for five days.'

'What the hell's that got to do with you?'

In fact, a lonely Mrs Swan, whose husband, Fred, was away working on an oil-rig supply

Alex Dewar gives the benefit of his advice to Betty Swan.

vessel, had been spending the weekend with self-styled hypnotherapist Alex Dewar at his holiday cottage on the west coast. They had first met at a disco on the Clyde Walkway, Havana Joe's, where Dewar's young lodger, Scott Adair, played drums with a group called The Rivals.

Another day – and Taggart was no nearer discovering the identity of the corpse. Late that night, he was sitting alone in his office, pondering his predicament. Relations with Jean were strained. Wearily, he lifted out the file on Angus Robinson and picked up a card which Robinson said he had found behind his clock. The card read: *Alexander Dewar, Hypnotherapist.*

Taggart decided that he and Livingstone should pay a visit on Mr Dewar. They were confronted with a dapper man in his early forties, someone who was clearly attracted to, and held an attraction for, women. Taggart recognized him as the man who had driven Betty Swan home. He proceeded to quiz the smooth-talking Dewar about the missing Mary Robinson.

'We understand she was a patient of yours …'

'Yes. Her husband was here yesterday.'

'When did you last see her?'

Dewar consulted a large red book. 'April the twenty-seventh.'

'Mrs Robinson went missing on the twenty-eighth.'

'I didn't realize.'

'So anything you can tell us about her would be useful.'

Dewar sat down. 'She was depressed. Unhappy with her family. Felt trapped. I meet a lot of women like her.'

Livingstone interjected. 'Would she have taken her own life?'

'I don't know,' replied Dewar. 'I hope not.'

'Did she tell you she intended leaving her husband and children?'

'No. But if she had, it wouldn't have surprised me.'

'Where did Mrs Robinson find out about your services?' persisted Livingstone.

'I advertise.'

Taggart stepped in. 'Was Mrs Swan a patient?'

'No. She was just a friend.'

Taggart noticed a pair of shoes on the floor. 'Are you married, Mr Dewar?'

'Separated. My wife's living in France, I think.'

'How long ago?'

'About a year.'

The significance of the questions began to dawn on Dewar. 'Is this the same enquiry – are you still looking for the owner of the legs?'

'It is the same enquiry.'

Dewar was adamant. 'I wouldn't chop up a woman … Terrible waste …'

Eager to trace the rug in which the legs were wrapped, Livingstone and Detective Sergeant Kenny Forfar sought out Rhona Cameron, proprietor of Cameron Woollens. Mrs Cameron, an attractive woman of thirty-eight, said that the only way to be sure that the rug was made at her mill would be to check through all the dyestuffs which were kept on file. Even then, the rug would have been on sale in hundreds of shops.

Taggart asked Mrs Cameron for a list of employees, present and recent. To avoid alerting her staff, she suggested he come to her house to collect the dyestuff. Taggart was only too happy to oblige. She kept horses. He found her interesting. She did not even flinch when told that the rug was used to wrap a human body. Obviously, she was a woman after his own heart.

Taggart was out bright and early the next morning. News had come through that another stockinged leg had been found, this time stuffed up a pipe on Milngavie golf course. Either the victim was a three-legged woman or there was a second body. But as Dr Andrews unwrapped the leg in his laboratory, he detected the smell of formalin, used as a preservative for biological specimens, particularly in medical departments of universities. The third leg was a hoax, planted by a couple of medical students, Tom and Andy. Taggart read the riot act to them, flatly refusing to allow them to go to the toilet. At the height of their discomfort, a call came in to report a genuine find. A human head had gone into the incinerator at Queenslie rubbish dump.

On his way out, Taggart instructed Livingstone: 'Keep those two in there another hour. Then let them go to the toilet.'

'You can't do that,' pleaded Livingstone.

Taggart was unmoved. 'I can do anything I want.'

At the same time, the lab reported a match on the dyes used in the rug. Forfar was dispatched to ask Mrs Cameron for a list of retail outlets while Taggart and Livingstone met Dr Andrews at the rubbish disposal depot. Since the incinerator had been burning for over seven hours, it would not have cooled down sufficiently for inspection until the following morning. The task of sifting through the 500 tons of rubbish was assigned to a team led by Livingstone and Forfar.

'What exactly will you be looking for?' asked the controller.

'A payrise,' answered Livingstone caustically.

'Will you be here on Sunday?'

'Yes,' said Livingstone.

'That's good. If Rangers get beat tomorrow, there'll be a few more bodies coming in for you.'

With that, the controller trotted off with a little smirk on his face. Livingstone didn't feel like sharing it.

Taggart had a more pleasant early morning rendezvous, renewing acquaintance with Rhona Cameron, who supplied him with a list of 250 stores in Strathclyde alone which sold the rug, plus the requested breakdown on her employees. The rug had been in production for five years, so it looked like being a long search. As they sat cosily in her kitchen, Taggart did not confine his questioning to the case.

'What does your husband do?'

'We're divorced,' answered Mrs Cameron, fingering her mug of coffee.

'How long?'

'Ten years now.'

'Perhaps you were too independent for him?' ventured Taggart.

She would not be drawn. 'Perhaps.'

That night, Taggart worked late at the office to accommodate Judy Morris,

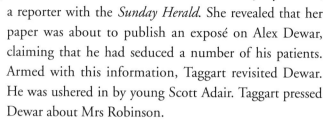

a reporter with the *Sunday Herald*. She revealed that her paper was about to publish an exposé on Alex Dewar, claiming that he had seduced a number of his patients. Armed with this information, Taggart revisited Dewar. He was ushered in by young Scott Adair. Taggart pressed Dewar about Mrs Robinson.

'Was she just a patient, Mr Dewar? Or did you try to get on friendlier terms?'

For the first time, Dewar lost his cool. 'What do you think I am?'

'Did you hypnotize her?'

McVitie, Taggart and Livingstone put their heads together over the mystery identity of the dismembered body.

'Yes.'

'Make a recording?'

'No.'

'Isn't that the usual procedure?'

Dewar became increasingly flustered. 'Sometimes I do. Sometimes I don't. In Mrs Robinson's case, I didn't.'

Taggart warmed to the task. 'I'm reliably informed that not all your consultations are, well, conducted professionally.'

'That's a damned insult. Who's been spreading this rubbish?'

'Never mind who's been spreading it.'

'I have a right to know,' demanded Dewar.

'And,' snapped Taggart, 'I have a right to know everything Mrs Robinson said! Depression. Family life. Sexual problems. Everything!'

Back at the rubbish depot, Livingstone confided to Taggart that they had another missing person to worry about. Kenny Forfar's wife, Jane, had walked out on him a week ago last Friday and had not been heard of since. Forfar had scoffed at the idea that she might be the murder victim.

Livingstone was beginning to fear that the search of the tip would produce nothing more than a personal hygiene problem until he pulled away a child's rusty pram and an object partially wrapped in a piece of MacDonald tartan rug rolled out at his feet. Closer inspection revealed two human arms.

However, Dr Andrews had bad news. 'Decomposition is no problem in itself,' he told Taggart and Livingstone. 'Fingerprints go right down to the dermis. In this case we have no dermis.'

'Eaten by maggots, Peter,' enthused Taggart.

Livingstone was beside himself. 'Two days in all that stinking rubbish and we don't even have her fingerprints. Fan-bloody-tastic.'

But Dr Andrews did make the point that the limbs seemed to have been very skilfully dismembered. 'Could be you're looking for a butcher …'

No sooner had the exposé on Alex Dewar appeared in the Scottish *Sunday Herald* than a posse of angry husbands turned up at his front door to exact retribution. Among them were Angus Robinson and Fred Swan, home from his stint on the oil rig. Dewar tried to persuade his lodger, Scott Adair, to help him confront the baying mob.

'It'll cost you a month's rent,' said Adair coldly.

'Two weeks,' insisted Dewar, attempting to bargain.

'Four – including the two I already I owe you.'

Dewar was furious at his friend's lack of loyalty. 'Get stuffed.'

Adair went to his room, leaving Dewar to face the music. Dewar refused to budge. Suddenly, a rock smashed through the parlour window. Dewar raced outside to remonstrate – just what the irate spouses wanted. Immediately, they grabbed him and beat him to the ground. Bloody and battered, he was only spared further punishment by the arrival of Livingstone, who, in endeavouring to break up the fracas, received a bloody nose from Fred Swan for his pains.

More than a week after the first find, the police still had no idea who the dead woman might be. McVitie, his proposed trip to Bali drawing nearer by the minute, was growing impatient. Acting on Dr Andrews' hunch, Taggart began quizzing local butchers. Among the businesses on his rounds was D. McSwean, Family Butcher. Taggart and Livingstone approached the proprietor, Dave McSwean.

'Mr McSwean?'

'You don't have to tell me,' replied McSwean, resignedly. 'I've had three other butchers on to me today already. You're looking for the guy who chopped up this woman.'

Livingstone got straight to the point. 'Are you married?'

''Fraid so.'

'Is your wife accounted for?'

'*Accounted for*. What kind of language is he speaking?'

Taggart translated. 'Is she at home?'

'If she's not,' said McSwean, 'give her a ballocking.' One of his female members of staff then confirmed that his wife was in the shop the previous afternoon. Another blank. Taggart desperately needed a break.

The break came as a result of a man out walking his dog along the side of a country stream. He became suspicious when the dog started sticking its nose into a bundle wrapped in a tartan rug. The smell was awful. He peered inside and discovered a human torso.

Livingstone crouched down to examine the bundle, all the while holding a handkerchief to his nose to avert the stench. Taggart scratched his head, contemplating. Just then, Livingstone spotted something. Gently, he reached into the folds of the rug and extracted a pigeon feather.

McVitie inspected the find. 'It could have got there since.'

'It was too deep inside,' said Livingstone.

At that moment, a young policeman ran towards them. 'We've got another body down the road,' he called out breathlessly. 'Lying in the ditch.'

'Shit!' exclaimed Taggart.

The police contingent made its way a hundred yards along the road. The second body, that of an elderly woman, was half hidden by scrub.

The police stumble across the body of a hit-and-run victim only yards from another grisly discovery ...

'She's a Mrs Harriet Gordon. Green Drive, Rutherglen,' announced Livingstone, a small leather wallet in his hand.

Dr Andrews stood up from examining the stricken woman. 'She's been dead for about three days. Looks like a particularly nasty hit-and-run. I suppose we're all thinking the same thing?'

Taggart concurred. 'He's made his first mistake.'

Dr Andrews got to work on the torso, establishing that the victim had been shot more than once.

'Now at least we know how she died,' sighed McVitie.

'Doesn't fit the pattern of domestic murder though, does it?' said Taggart.

'You must know quite a lot about your murderer now,' suggested Dr Andrews.

'We do,' said McVitie, looking pointedly at Taggart. 'Everything bar his name.'

At least they were able to eliminate one possible victim, when Livingstone received a phone call from Jane Forfar. She requested a secret meeting on Glasgow Green, after hearing that the police were looking for her, and proceeded to pour her heart out to Livingstone.

'It's not easy being a policeman's wife,' she sighed, nervously fingering her wedding ring. 'It's not just the hours. You can fill them. I was fed up – breathing the police force. Sleeping with it. Kenny's drinking didn't help either. I intend staying away, Peter. I don't want Kenny to find me. He'll only end up talking me into going back. And feeling sorry for somebody isn't any basis for a marriage.'

She handed Livingstone her wedding and engagement rings. 'There's one thing you can do. Give him those. I don't want them.'

Taggart and his men set about checking every pigeon owner in Glasgow. It was an onerous task – but preferable to scouring rubbish tips. They learned that the bullets were nine millimetre Italian Phiochi, more usually found abroad in personal protection guns. They were something of a novelty in Glasgow.

Comparing the list of pigeon keepers with Rhona Cameron's ex-employees, Taggart came up with a name which was on both – George Bryce. Three years ago, he had worked for four months as a packer at the woollen mill, so it was with some optimism that Taggart approached Bryce's suburban house. Bryce, a middle-aged man of around forty, who, considering his job, was curiously undernourished, was in the process of cleaning out the corrugated iron pigeon hut at the bottom of his garden.

'Mind if we have a few words?' asked Taggart.

'No,' said Bryce, glancing back with concern.

'Whereabouts do you work?' asked Livingstone.

'McSwean's … The butcher.'

'You're a butcher?' repeated Livingstone, realizing the implications.

Bryce became agitated. 'I make haggises, black puddings – it's a small business – we all do a bit of everything. I do deliveries as well.'

Taggart closed in. 'Is your wife at home?'

'No, we're separated. She's – I don't know where she is.'

'Sorry to hear that,' said Taggart, belying his true thoughts. 'How long has she been … gone?'

'About three months now.'

'Where did you work before McSwean's?'

'I had a few jobs. Filling in, sort of – after I was made redundant.'

'Redundant from where?'

'Where I used to work. In the slaughterhouse.'

It was getting better by the minute.

Taggart and Livingstone's enquiries take them closer to the Clyde.

As they left, Taggart pointed out the dent in the bonnet of Bryce's car. A perfect fit for the hit-and-run? Taggart certainly thought so. 'We've got him!' he exclaimed tight-lipped when they were out of Bryce's earshot.

Back in McVitie's office, Taggart and Livingstone presented their findings. McVitie passed them a report which stated that fawn-coloured paint had been found on the victim of the hit-and-run. Livingstone was all for pulling in Bryce there and then but Taggart wanted to wait for further forensic tests. In the meantime, he would let Bryce stew.

Taggart wasted little time in finding a reason to visit Rhona Cameron again, and requested all records of discount sales to staff in the hope that Bryce might have bought a tartan rug. The following morning, Taggart decided it was time to bring Bryce in for questioning. He arrived at McSwean's, only to be told that Bryce was dead. He had been shot the previous evening while preparing haggises in the butchery.

Taggart and Livingstone glanced down at the body.

Taggart was stunned. 'What do we have, Peter?'

'If Bryce killed his wife, who killed Bryce?'

Taggart shook his head. 'The Biscuit is not going to like this ...'

Forfar and Livingstone quizzed Rosy French and Jessie Clark, two women who worked for McSwean. Rosy, the younger of the pair, had only been there for two weeks and had been making a play for Bryce. Taggart meanwhile interrogated McSwean, who revealed that Bryce had stayed behind the night before to catch up with some work and also to meet somebody. McSwean added that whoever killed him must have turned out the lights and locked up.

The only definite progress was that the torso in the rug was not that of Mrs Robinson. She had sent Angus a postcard from Majorca, announcing that she had no intention of coming back.

Taggart and Livingstone took over the questioning of Rosy, concentrating on her relationship with Bryce.

'We weren't close or anything. I felt sorry for him. His wife had left him, and his daughter was dead.

'He never mentioned a daughter,' said Taggart, puzzled.

'She died of a drug overdose sometime last year,' said Rosy.

On one visit to Bryce's house, Rosy remembered meeting a strange young man in the doorway of the basement. Pressed for a description, she offered to draw the mystery visitor. She also recalled that he was wearing a lapel badge with some sort of slogan.

A search of Bryce's living room produced one surprising item – an old publicity photo of The Rivals, signed by each member of the band.

Livingstone said he had seen them at Havana Joe's.

The tension of the case was beginning to get to everyone. McVitie was going around like a bear with a sore head, Taggart was in trouble because he had been unable to join Jean on her working trip to Canada and Forfar and Livingstone came to blows at Havana Joe's when Forfar realized that Livingstone had been in touch with his wife.

McVitie, whose mood was not improved by the sight of Livingstone's black eye, reported that the bullets which killed the woman and Bryce had been fired from the same gun. On McVitie's desk lay the artist's impression drawn by Rosy. Taggart immediately recognized him as Alex Dewar's lodger, Scott Adair. Taggart and Livingstone made straight for Dewar's house, where Dewar told them that Adair had left in a hurry.

'Do you know if he ever met a man called George Bryce?' asked Taggart.

Dewar thought for a moment. 'He had a girlfriend once called Pauline Bryce …'

While the search was on for Scott Adair, who had been sacked from The Rivals, Taggart sought inspiration in the company of George Bryce's pigeons. He felt sorry for them locked in their cage and coaxed a couple out of their dookit. As he brought them out into the daylight, with the intention of feeding them, a woman of about forty approached him, carrying a suitcase. It was Edna Bryce, George's wife – very much alive. Mrs Bryce had been working at a hotel in Edinburgh but had read of George's murder.

'Did you know your daughter's boyfriend – Scott Adair?' asked Taggart.

'Yes. I haven't seen him since the trial.'

'What trial was this?'

'There was a relief teacher called Heather Jameson. Accused of drug dealing. Scott told us that she had sold Pauline the drugs that killed her.'

'How did he know that?'

'They all went to this disco.'

'Not Havana Joe's?'

'That was it,' said Mrs Bryce. 'It's so wrong. George and Pauline dead. And she's still free.'

'I hardly think she's that, Mrs Bryce.' Taggart was certain he had finally put a name to his torso in the tartan rug.

Livingstone talked to members of the drug squad about the Jameson case, for which the jury had returned a verdict of not proven, allowing the accused to walk free. The drugs officers remembered a lot of angry parents threatening to kill Jameson, particularly a guy called Fred Swan, whose son had died in a motorcycle accident. The lad had been on LSD at the time, supplied by

Heather Jameson.

In Jean's absence, Taggart asked Rhona Cameron to dinner. She had already furnished him with the information that George Bryce had indeed purchased a discount rug, but her next words were less welcome.

'You're wasting your time with me,' she said, trying to let him down gently. 'Why?'

She took a deep breath. 'I was married once. Because it was what my family expected. Now I'm free. And next to horses, I prefer my own sex.'

Taggart made his excuses and left.

Livingstone's enquiries proved more fruitful. He made contact with the Officer of the Watch on the oil-rig supply boat, MV Braemar, to check Fred Swan's movements. The log-book contained a record of three ship-to-shore calls – made by Swan to Bryce's number. Bryce and Swan had both been present at Jameson's trial.

'I know who killed Bryce,' Livingstone told McVitie excitedly. 'It wasn't Scott Adair. At the time the woman was killed, Fred Swan's ship was up the Clyde for repairs. It makes sense – Swan did the shooting, and Bryce was left to dispose of the body because Swan had to go back to sea. The hit-and-run victim had seen Bryce dump the torso.'

George Bryce gets the final chop in his butchery.

'Scott Adair, is he in it at all?' asked McVitie.

'He must be.'

'You mean – all three of them?'

'Looks like it.'

'Jim know about Swan?'

'Eh, no!' replies Livingstone, quietly pleased with himself but sensing that a full-blooded gloat could damage his prospects of promotion.

'You'll be popular …'

The police homed in on Swan. He had gone to Havana Joe's to seek out Scott Adair. Swan tried to entice Adair outside.

'Don't you read the papers? Your face is all over them. Come on.'

Adair resisted. 'I'm not going with you.'

'Do you want to be recognized?'

'So what if I am? I didn't kill her – I just found her for you.'

'But you know, son,' warned Swan, his voice heavy with menace.

'You can't get me in here,' gabbled Adair. 'Like George. I'm safe in here.'

Adair decided the safest place of all was in the spotlight so he hastily reclaimed his old spot on the drums with The Rivals. Swan retreated to a dark corner. Spotting the arrival of Taggart, Swan knew that time was at a premium. He crept into the disc jockey's booth and turned up the smoke machine. It would provide the perfect camouflage for murder. Adair became alarmed. He could no longer see Swan clearly. But through the ever-thickening dry ice, he could just make out Swan reaching into his pocket. Before he could move, a bullet crashed into the cymbal. Adair made a break for it across the dance-floor but was apprehended by Taggart. More muffled shots. Swan, the gun and silencer returned to his pocket, headed purposefully for the door.

He flashed his Merchant Navy ID card to the bouncers. 'Police. Open the door but don't let anybody else out.'

A voice rang out from the back of the crowd. 'Stop that man! He's the one! He's got a gun!'

Swan pulled the gun but was instantly wrestled to the ground by two burly bouncers. As the gun fell, Taggart, himself wounded, lay on the floor. A few feet away, Scott Adair lay motionless, face down.

'There's an ambulance on its way,' said Livingstone, crouching down.

'Tell Jean – I won't make it,' mumbled Taggart.

'You'll make it,' said Livingstone, reassuringly, tending the wound.

Even in pain, Taggart despaired of his young sergeant. 'To Canada, you dunderheid.'

THE KILLING PHILOSOPHY

Taggart reviews the evidence surrounding the vicious assault of Mary Imrie.

Transmission dates:
15–29 April 1987
Writer: Glenn Chandler
Producer: Robert Love
Director: Haldane Duncan

SUPPORTING CAST:
DET. CON. MIKE JARDINE
– James Macpherson
KIM REDMOND
– Sheila Grier
PATRICK CLARK
– Philip Dupuy
ALAN MCMASTERS
– Richard Jamieson
JOHN LANG
– Paul Kiernan
KEVIN REDMOND
– Rod Culbertson
SYLVANA WATSON
– Kika Mirylees
ERNIE GALLAGHER
– Kenneth Bryans
JOAN RAEBURN
– Jenny Lee

It was a typically quiet suburban morning along the tree-lined avenues in the smart Bearsden district of Glasgow, the silence broken only by the singing of the birds and the sound of car engines starting up in preparation for the daily migration to the city offices. A paper-boy ambled along the road with customary sloth, delivering the news at his leisure.

Suddenly, he was jerked from his lethargy when he was unable to push the paper through the letterbox of one house. Something seemed to be blocking it. He looked around and spotted a broken window. It was clearly a matter for the police.

This was no ordinary burglary. The occupant, Mary Imrie, a woman of forty, had been the victim of a vicious attempted rape, perpetrated by a man in a dark leather mask. Taggart and young Detective Constable Mike Jardine arrived on the scene, accompanied by policewoman Laura Campbell. They found Mary, the side of her face badly bruised, tightly clutching an old rag doll with no eyes.

Taggart surveyed the state of the house. The fridge door was open and across the kitchen floor stretched a trail of opened packets of biscuits, cheese and cake. A tin of beans had been opened and spooned out, cans of lemonade had been drunk from. It looked as though someone had been having a picnic. Taggart moved into the lounge, a room lit only by the thin rays of sunlight filtering in through the closed curtains. The settee had been upended and placed against the window where, in conjunction with other items of moved furniture, it had formed a crude barricade. A sideboard had been similarly set against the door in the hall, thus causing the obstruction to the letterbox.

One piece of furniture had not been touched in the lounge – the dining table. It remained set for two, complete with the leftovers from a candlelit dinner. On the table were candlesticks with candles which had burnt low, two empty wine bottles and an empty champagne bottle. It had been quite a feast.

Still in a state of shock and with the doll nearby, Mary relived her ordeal for Taggart and DC Campbell in the special rape suite of Maryhill police station. She tried to remember what she could about her attacker. It was a struggle to force out the words.

'His clothes were all black. They smelt old – stale. He was just waiting for me. Downstairs. Waiting. He turned off the lights at the mains. He tried to …'

While Campbell comforted her, Taggart asked Mary whom she had been entertaining for dinner. Mary confirmed that her guest was a married man, but flatly refused to divulge his name.

'Is he that important, sir?' asked Campbell, trying to spare Mary further pain.

'Aye, it's important.'

'Please …'

Taggart would not back down. 'We need to eliminate him, Mary.'

Mary's eyes raced around the room. She had a haunted look. 'You don't believe me, do you? None of you believe me.'

'Course we do,' said Taggart. 'We just want to talk to him.'

Taggart's tactics upset Campbell. She collared him in the corridor afterwards. 'Chief Inspector, it's the policy of the female and child unit to believe rape victims – not bully them and suggest they're lying.'

'I wanted the name, that's all,' said Taggart.

Campbell would not be appeased. 'You think she's making it up? About the masked man?'

'She might have good reason to.'

'The furniture – the broken window – you think she did all that?'

'She could be covering up for him,' suggested Jardine. 'Romantic dinner – he misinterprets the invitation.'

Campbell was livid. 'Oh, I suppose that would make it all right!'

Mary's mystery boyfriend was quickly eliminated. Red roses found strewn about the lounge were traced to a florist in Rutherglen, who described the purchaser as forty, pushing sixty, and not exactly in the physical condition needed for shifting furniture. A more feasible suspect seemed to be convicted rapist Martin Caldwell, who had escaped from Carstairs prison on the night of Mary's attack and who used to live in the Bearsden area.

Any lingering doubts Taggart may have harboured about Mary Imrie's story vanished a week later when librarian Joan Raeburn, a woman living alone in Bearsden, was attacked in her home in the early hours of the morning by the same man. The *modus operandi* was identical – the expert entry through a small window, the food dragged from the fridge, the furniture barricaded against the door, the lights switched off at the mains. Joan had been sitting in bed reading when the lights went out. Going downstairs to carry out repairs, she came across the barricade of furniture. She immediately retreated to her absent son's bedroom to arm herself with a cricket bat. It was a blow from the bat, delivered across the back of his neck, which sent the intruder fleeing and spared Joan any further ordeal. The description of the man tallied with the previous incident. He wore black clothes and a full-face leather mask with a slit for the eyes.

MARTIN CALDWELL
– Hamish Reid
DET. CON. LAURA CAMPBELL
– Patricia Ross
MARY IMRIE
– Gerda Stevenson
BILL BRUCE
– Michael MacKenzie
PAUL FRASER
– Peter Raffan
MARTIN KENNEDY
– William Armour

Joan Raeburn said that she would never forget those eyes – the way they bored through her. She was certain she could recognize them again. Back at the station, she looked through countless sets of eyes, including those belonging to Martin Caldwell. Taggart and Livingstone anxiously awaited her reaction. There was none. She was unable to make a positive identification.

'Is that it, then?' she said. 'I'll be at the library if you need me. Can't stay off work because of an incident like this.'

'Good for you,' said Livingstone.

'Glad you think so,' said Joan. '*He* was the brave one, coming into my house.'

The discovery of a lair at nearby Possil Loch, where someone had been living rough, reinforced Taggart's suspicions about Caldwell. For among the items found was a shirt identical to the one Caldwell was wearing when he escaped. Could the musty smell described by Mary Imrie have come from her attacker living rough?

By now, Joan Raeburn's cricketing prowess had been splashed across the front pages, much to the irritation of Livingstone, who sought her out in the library accompanied by Mike Jardine.

'Supposing this prompted someone to emulate him?' he told her.

Joan, a single-minded woman who gave the impression that she enjoyed

Librarian Joan Raeburn, the intended second victim, escaped from her ordeal unhurt but is convinced she would always remember her attacker's eyes...

imposing library fines, was amazed at his tone. 'Glasgow's full of people who like being hit by cricket bats?'

As Livingstone and Jardine were about to leave, Joan picked up a book on archery. It prompted her to remember something else about the man in black.

'You know I said he had some burglary tool in his hand? Now I know what it was. It wasn't a tool. It was a small bow.'

Back at the station, Livingstone headed straight for the files. 'Ernie Gallagher. Housebreaking – same sort of entry and exit technique. Also, poaching deer out of season – with a crossbow.'

McVitie examined the file.

'He's not a rapist though,' protested Taggart.

'How do you know?' asked Livingstone.

'Because he's an old customer of mine.'

'What's to stop him starting?' said McVitie. 'Check him out. These two attacks happened within a mile of my house, Jim.'

'That'll bring down the rateable value,' muttered Taggart.

Taggart and Livingstone found Gallagher enjoying a peaceful afternoon's fishing. An inspection of his back failed to reveal any bruising. He had not been on the receiving end of Joan Raeburn's square cut.

Taggart's thoughts returned to Caldwell. He asked Livingstone to check out Sergeant-Major John Lang, who had been in the same Territorial Army regiment as Caldwell, and who kept guns, swords and crossbows at his home in Bearsden. Lang, a man of forty-five with a moustache and military bearing, lived in a large house guarded by a pair of snarling Dobermanns. He disclosed that he had been responsible for Caldwell's dismissal from the Territorials.

'It was me who caught him stealing money,' said Lang. 'Annual camp.'

'Did he ever train with a crossbow?' asked Livingstone.

Lang was dismissive. 'They're not much use against cruise missiles.'

'He'd have had weapons training though?' persisted Livingstone.

'Sure. He would have made a good soldier if he hadn't gone off the rails.'

'Have you seen him since?'

'Once. He came round and did my garden for me.'

'Your garden?'

'This was before Carstairs. He found out I lived near him – came round. Offered to do my garden for me. Said he needed the money. He wasn't much good, so we just forgot about it.'

'You trusted him?' said Livingstone, incredulous.

'I trust my dogs. I was giving him a chance.'

Suddenly things began to go disastrously wrong for Taggart. Mary Imrie never recovered from her experience and committed suicide on the railway line near her house; a police raid on the Possil Loch hide-out unearthed nothing more sinister than a birdwatcher; and the masked intruder struck for a third time.

A neighbour had noticed a broken toilet window in a large detached house in Bearsden belonging to Mrs Anne Bruce, an osteopath. Inside, Taggart, Livingstone and Jardine were greeted with a familiar picture – furniture barricaded against the doors and the contents of the fridge littered across the kitchen floor. While Livingstone was checking upstairs for any sign of Mrs Bruce, Taggart heard a plaintive miaowing coming from a closed cupboard beneath the stairs. As he opened the door, a black cat slipped out. Taggart crouched down and stroked it. His hand came away covered in blood. He opened the cupboard further and shone a penlight torch inside. There, amongst the household bric-à-brac, the light picked out a human body.

It was that of Mrs Bruce. She had been stabbed in the eyes and throat with a crossbow bolt. She had also been raped. Dr Andrews warned that a sexual psychopath was on the loose.

Mr Bruce had been away in Edinburgh at the time, but his outward show of indifference to his wife's murder led Taggart to probe deeper into the state of the Bruces' marriage. Could Bill Bruce have carried out the two previous attacks in order to deflect attention from the real aim – the killing of his wife? The name of Ernie Gallagher also cropped up again after his white transit van had been seen in the vicinity at 1am, an hour before the murder. Once more, the search proved fruitless.

With McVitie complaining that panic was sweeping through Bearsden like a bush fire, Taggart was forced to accept help from any quarter. This included Sylvana Watson, a stunningly attractive psychic medium in her thirties, whose trademark was huge pendulum-like earrings.

'I've tried three times to talk to you,' she said, sitting in Taggart's office. 'It's easier getting through to the dead.'

She offered to help Taggart track down Martin Caldwell. 'I thought if I could hold something that belonged to him – or study some crime scene photos – I might be able to tell you his whereabouts.'

'That simple,' replied Taggart.

'I wouldn't say simple. What have you to lose? A few minutes of time. And you've been searching for him for three weeks. There is one very strong feeling I get. His eyes are very important.'

'His eyes?'

'Yes. They somehow matter to this case. Very strongly.'

The mysterious killer, sensationally dubbed 'The Glasgow Bowman' by the press, had captured the public's fear and imagination in equal parts. After Livingstone and Jardine had been sent to investigate reports of a man seen practising with a crossbow in Garscadden Wood, Taggart returned home to find that a worried Jean had called out Paul Fraser of FAS Alarm and Security Services. With the bowman at large, she had repeatedly urged Taggart to improve security at their house. Taggart was not impressed when Fraser labelled both the house – and Jean – as particularly vulnerable.

'Is your business doing well, Mr Fraser?' he asked gruffly.

'Especially now, yes.'

'Who said crime doesn't pay?'

A breakthrough looked on the cards when Mrs McVitie, of all people, said that Bruce's secretary, who was with him in Edinburgh on the fateful night, had moved into the house the day after his wife's murder. What's more, Bruce was off to the States for a month. Taggart wasted no time in hauling him along to the station, encouraged by Joan Raeburn's assertion that she could identify her attacker by his eyes. As Bruce arrived at the station, Taggart made sure that Joan got a good look at him. Nothing.

The young Mike Jardine cut his teeth on the case of The Glasgow Bowman.

A week after the murder of Mrs Bruce, The Glasgow Bowman struck again. In the dead of night, he broke into a detached house in Bearsden. The female occupant, a girl of about twenty, managed to escape but her father was fatally wounded, left lying in the road, his pyjamas soaked with blood. At the front of the garden, police uncovered a pistol crossbow bolt with blood on it.

Bolt in hand, Taggart visited a city centre hunting shop, run by Martin Kennedy, in an attempt to trace the weapon.

'Yes, we sell this type,' said Kennedy.

'So,' confirmed Taggart, 'it's odds on that if it was bought in Glasgow, it was bought here?'

'We are the only stockists in Glasgow.'

Taggart tried to find out whether there had been any customers who smelt or had staring eyes – but without success. Before leaving, he appealed to Kennedy's public-spiritedness.

'Would you mind not selling any more of these things until we catch him? Don't want any neds running about playing Rambo.'

'Who'll reimburse me?' demanded the shop owner. 'This is my business.'

Taggart looked round at the display of guns. 'And I can think of a dozen

Horrified, a young woman leans over the fatally wounded body of her father, the latest victim of The Glasgow Bowman.

ways to make it hard for you to run!'

McVitie and Livingstone still felt that the fugitive Caldwell was their man, but Taggart expressed serious reservations. 'I arrested Caldwell. He came like a lamb. He said he needed help. He was just a boy in trouble, not a sadist.'

McVitie attempted to introduce a behavioural psychologist 'to back up Caldwell's psychiatrist. They're very fashionable in America.'

'We're not in America,' growled Taggart.

Livingstone disagreed. 'We are the same in cases like this.'

'That's right,' said McVitie. 'We cut our teeth on a different kind of crime. Society's changed. Now we have the random killer. The thrill killer. We have to listen to psychiatrists.'

Taggart was unmoved. 'I may have to listen to them in court. No other place.'

After days scouring Garscadden Wood, the hapless Jardine finally came up with something. Turning away from a courting couple, his attention was caught by an object at the base of a tree. It was an old round paper target, full of holes, similar in size to those made by a crossbow bolt. Next to it in the grass lay an empty bottle of Gazelle lager. It turned out to be a specially imported lager from Kenya Breweries, available in only one bar in the whole of Glasgow – Lowe's Bar, a renowned gay haunt. With a degree of malicious pleasure, Taggart ordered Livingstone and Jardine to go undercover to Lowe's.

The operation produced an unexpected result when Livingstone received a call from Sergeant-Major Lang, who had seen him at the gay bar. Lang invited Livingstone to his house, ostensibly to demonstrate his fencing technique. When it became apparent that Lang had other designs, Livingstone was forced to beat a hasty retreat.

Meanwhile, impressed by personal information she had sent him about his own background, Taggart decided to take up the offer of help from Sylvana Watson. As she spread her hands out over the scene of crime photographs, she began to receive a picture of the killer. 'I see a man. He watches. He waits. He stakes out his victims. Always I come back to his eyes. He has something to do with education – perhaps to do with a university.' Fascinating perhaps, but her profile did not fit in with any of Taggart's suspects.

Then, over four weeks after the attack on Mary Imrie, Martin Caldwell at last broke cover by sending a letter to the *Evening Times*. In it, he categorically stated that he was not The Glasgow Bowman. On his way to the newspaper offices to examine the letter, Taggart spotted a group of football supporters carrying a banner proclaiming: THERE'S ONLY ONE GLASGOW BOWMAN. Livid at the glorification of a cold-hearted killer, Taggart seized the banner and screwed it up.

'Is this Russia or something?' screamed one of the gang. 'That took me three hours!'

Taggart bridled. 'You think he's some kind of hero? Suppose his next victim was your mother. Your sister. Maybe your girlfriend!

His little speech was wasted. As the mob set off along the street, they broke into a chant. 'There's only one Glasgow Bowman … one Glasgow Bowman.'

At the *Evening Times*, Livingstone made the most of the news editor's sudden absence by studying the postmark on Caldwell's letter.

'N-wood. N-wood?'

'Thornwood!' said Taggart excitedly.

The presence of grain dust on the envelope led them to an old granary on the banks of the Clyde. Taggart went in alone. The scruffy, unshaven Caldwell was huddled in a disused office. Suddenly, he heard Taggart's footsteps and pulled out a knife.

Taggart called out. 'Martin. Martin.'

Caldwell saw Taggart through a maze of pillars and put the knife away. He tried to disguise his presence by covering the smell of the fish and chips which he had been eating with a jacket. Taggart's nostrils were too sensitive, however.

'Hello, Martin.'

Caldwell stepped out into the open. 'Mr Taggart. How did you find me?'

'You wanted to be found. Otherwise, you wouldn't have shoved that letter over a post office counter.'

'I've done nothing.'

'Some people think differently.'

'Suppose I stay here and only we know. You can tell them I'm safe. I got out to prove I'm cured. I can live like anybody else. I can prove I'm safe. I don't need that place. Not any more.'

'Martin, you still need treatment.'

'Five more years? They won't let me out. Not ever. I'll be like them. Here, I have a chance.'

'Here? Live like an animal, Martin? What'll that prove? Suppose you come with me now – quietly – that'll be worth more than a year living here.'

Caldwell considered the proposition. 'Will you tell them?'

Taggart nodded. 'I'll tell them.'

Receiving such an assurance, Caldwell gave himself up.

If proof were needed that Caldwell was not the Bowman, it came the following night. With Caldwell in custody, the killer appeared to have struck once more. This time the victim was Kevin Redmond, a man in his mid-thirties. Taggart and Livingstone arrived to find his hysterical wife, Kim, surrounded by the hallmarks of scattered food and furniture. The body lay in the kitchen of their bungalow, the face twisted to the side next to an opened, half-empty tin of beans. A couple of feet away lay a blood-soaked tea-towel.

'It's him alright,' said Livingstone.

Taggart went up to the Redmonds' bedroom. On the floor by the bed side he noticed a key. He picked it up and placed it in a protective envelope.

He returned to the kitchen, where Dr Andrews was concluding his examination of the corpse.

'No sign of a bolt?' said Dr Andrews.

'Not this time,' replied Taggart. 'Not yet.'

'Injury's consistent with one,' confirmed the pathologist. 'Entry and exit wounds, probably penetrating the jugular. Causing air embolism.'

'Would he have died immediately?'

'Not necessarily. Could have clung on for up to an hour. Curiously, there seems to be congestion in his mouth that I'd associate more with asphyxia.'

At the Maryhill station rape suite, Taggart and Laura Campbell questioned Kim Redmond, an attractive blonde in a faded showgirl kind of way. She ran a local dancing school.

'His eyes – they stared right through me,' said Kim, doing her best to keep her composure. 'He was wearing a mask, made of leather, and army clothes – they smelt as though they hadn't been washed.'

'You say he attacked Kevin in the bedroom?' asked Campbell.

'Yes. Kevin tried to fight him off. And then he came after me. I brought my knee up, like they say you should. And then he ran away in pain – out the bathroom window. I think that was the way he got in. Then I phoned you.'

Taggart produced the key on the fob. 'Do you recognize these keys?'

'No.'

'We found it beside the bed.'

'Oh, they must be for the old lock on the front door. Kevin changed it – because of this man …'

Campbell looked thoughtful as she emerged from the interview.

'What's on your mind?' asked Taggart.

'I don't quite believe her. I'm not sure why.'

Taggart grinned triumphantly. 'I thought it was the policy of the unit *always* to believe the victim of a rape or attempted rape.'

Livingstone comforts Kim Redmond when the body of her husband, Kevin, is discovered in the kitchen.

Livingstone continued to frequent Lowe's Bar that lunchtime. He was intrigued to see a young man in a camouflage jacket come in and order Gazelle lager. He sidled up to him and made conversation.

'I'll get that,' offered Livingstone. 'Do you always drink that stuff?'

'I like it.'

Livingstone introduced himself and discovered that his new acquaintance was Alan McMasters, a student at Glasgow University. What's more, the sudden entry of Lang made it patently obvious that McMasters was his boyfriend. The army clothes, the lager, the access to Lang's crossbows were enough to whet Taggart's appetite, but the news that McMasters was a university student made him positively ravenous. Remembering Sylvana Watson's words, he arranged for McMasters to take part in an identity parade. Neither Kim Redmond nor Joan Raeburn could identify him. Another dead end.

But as they returned to Taggart's office, Joan Raeburn had an admission to make. 'I didn't want to let you down. The truth is, I couldn't see properly downstairs.'

'Don't you wear glasses?' said Livingstone.

'I'm wearing my contact lenses. Vanity, I suppose. It's the first time in a month. I thought I'd lost the right one but I found it when I was hoovering the chairs in the living room. But I can't see out of it properly.'

Taggart asked to have a look at them. 'The tints are different,' he observed. He thought for a moment. 'When you were talking about hoovering round the chair – when you hit that guy with the cricket bat, was he standing by that chair?'

'Come to think of it, yes, he was.'

All energies were now concentrated on finding the owner of the lens. A tour of opticians eventually paid off. It belonged to Kevin Redmond, the man who was supposedly the most recent victim of The Glasgow Bowman.

Taggart and Livingstone searched the converted garden shed where Redmond worked as an engraver. Taggart noticed a sturdy box beneath the lathe.

Kevin Redmond: the last victim of The Glasgow Bowman?

'What's in that?' he asked Kim.

'I don't know. I never interfered with Kevin's things.'

Taggart opened the box. Inside he found a bundle of dark, smelly clothing, a leather mask, a collection of pornographic magazines and a pistol crossbow. Kevin Redmond was the Bowman.

Kim recoiled in horror. 'No! He just couldn't be. He was impotent.'

Taggart was philosophical. 'Maybe he just needed this for that extra thrill.'

So who killed Kevin Redmond? The answer was quickly supplied by Alan McMasters. When Kim Redmond had attended the identity parade, she had accidentally snagged the black curtain separating herself from the line-up, thereby allowing McMasters to catch a glimpse of her. He had seen her many times before. His friend, fellow philosophy student Patrick Clark, had been having a long-standing affair with Mrs Redmond. It annoyed McMasters, who wanted Clark for himself. Now McMasters saw his chance for revenge. A crossbow had gone missing from John Lang's collection shortly before Redmond's murder and McMasters realized that his personal key to Lang's house was also missing. The last time he had it was when he was sitting next to Clark in the tutorial room. Putting two and two together, he concluded that Clark must have taken the key from his pocket, broken into Lang's house, stolen one of the crossbows and killed Redmond.

McMasters confronted Clark with his suspicions. 'I want the key to John's house and I want to know where that crossbow is.'

With a confidence born of good looks, Clark tried to bluff his way out but sensed that his friend knew too much. 'I don't have it here. It's hidden.'

'I want it, Patrick.'

'You're in a strong position,' admitted Clark. 'You could have anything off me you wanted. And you've always wanted me, haven't you? Now's your chance. Why don't you demand it?'

McMasters dismissed the suggestion. 'I've too much decency.'

Clark paused for a moment to consider his next move. Then he announced: 'It's under the Kingston Bridge.'

An hour later, McMasters phoned the police. Taggart, Livingstone and Jardine drove straight for the Kingston Bridge. They were not in time to prevent another death. For that evening in the grim wasteland beneath the bridge, Clark planned to silence his friend for good with an iron bar. McMasters managed to avoid the blow. In desperation, he pulled a knife on the advancing Clark. There was a struggle. The knife dropped into the Clyde. Clark now held the upper hand and tried to drown McMasters by holding his head beneath the murky waters. With a supreme effort, McMasters succeeded in retrieving the knife. Clark maintained the pressure on his neck. Suddenly Clark's expression of triumphant determination changed dramatically. He realized he had been stabbed in the chest. He rolled over, blood soaking into his shirt, as the police arrived on the scene. Taggart and Livingstone crouched over the stricken Clark. Before he died, he managed a faint smile.

Kim Redmond turns out not to be what she appears...

The rest of the story soon unfolded. Although it had been Clark's idea to murder Kevin Redmond and, ironically, to copy the methods of The Glasgow Bowman, Kim Redmond was a willing accomplice. She not only admitted Clark to the bungalow but also, when her husband still showed signs of life, with the police at the front door, it was she who had finished him off by asphyxiating him with the tea-towel.

'She could certainly pick her men,' reflected Livingstone.

'Eye for an eye, Peter,' said Taggart, knowingly.

'Wonder what she saw in him?'

'Two things you should never try to understand. The mind of a murderer and the mind of a woman.'

'Sexist!'

Taggart almost cracked open a smile. 'There's still some of us left!'

EVIL EYE

The unfortunate
Euphemia Lambie
(played by Maggie
Bell, the voice
behind the series'
theme song).

Murder sites are rarely picturesque, but this one seemed a particularly unappealing place to spend the morning. It was a gypsy site in Firhill. The victim, Euphemia Lambie, a mother of four, had been killed the previous night. Her children, Jimmy, Petrina and the two younger ones, Maggie and Robert, were less than forthcoming. And the other member of the family, affectionately known as Grandpa Willy, was senile. All Taggart could glean at first was that the kids had returned to find her dead in the caravan. The arrival of Dr Andrews speeded up the investigation. He paid close attention to the dead woman's right hand, on which the fingers and thumbs were 'steepled' together.

He turned to Taggart. 'She was stabbed twice, once in the chest, once lower down in the abdomen. Both wounds capable of being fatal. Rigor is fully established – she died some time yesterday, say between three in the afternoon and eleven in the evening. She's been dead about seventeen hours. And she's been moved, laid out.' He gestured to her right hand. 'The right hand is interesting. Seems to have undergone what we call cadaveric spasm. A violent spasm of the muscles that makes it go stiff at the moment of death. The fingers seem to have been holding something, but there's nothing in them. Oh, and the other hand had rings on too, but they've been pulled off. Roughly.'

Transmission dates:
4–18 September 1990
Writer: Glenn Chandler
Producer: Robert Love
Director: Haldane Duncan

SUPPORTING CAST:
JANE ANTROBUS
– Jill Gascoine
FRANK ROURKE
– Johnny Beattie
DET. SGT. TILLING
– Gary Webster
DET. CHIEF INSP. MCGARRY
– John McGlynn
BILLY GALLOWAY
– Sam Graham
MALCOLM DURIE
– David O'Hara
DANNY BONNAR
– John Hannah

'Can you tell me anything about the knife that was used?' asked Taggart.

'I can't tell you the depth of the wounds yet. But I'd say the knife had a single cutting edge.'

Taggart showed him a knife in a protective bag. 'Would that have done it?'

'That could.'

Taggart took the knife down to the car, where Jimmy Lambie was being guarded by another detective. Taggart produced the knife.

'Is that your knife?'

'Aye,' replied Jimmy.

'It was found in the bus,' said Taggart sombrely. 'It's got blood on the hilt. Can you explain that?'

'I use it to skin rabbits.'

Just then, Jardine returned from questioning Tom Watt, a man in his fifties, who ran an unofficial gypsy site further along the road. Jardine was keen to establish the Lambie caravan's movements.

He reported back to Taggart. 'They only arrived *there* this morning.'

'What do you mean – there?'

'They brought the body there this morning,' explained Jardine. 'The guy didn't want us sniffing around so he sent them along here.'

For once, Taggart was at a loss for words. Then he turned to Jimmy. 'How many places has this body been to!'

It transpired that Euphemia Lambie had actually been murdered at a third gypsy site, some miles away on the outskirts of Glasgow. Taggart suspected that one of the family, until Petrina revealed that over £7,000 in cash plus a quantity of jewellery was missing from the caravan. A search of the murder site produced evidence of a car having recently skidded off the road and into the nearby river. There were also traces of fresh green paint on a broken fencing post, probably from the car, and, in the river, a diamond earring.

Taggart and Jardine tried to obtain a formal identification of the jewellery from Jimmy and Petrina. It was like getting blood out of a stone. The pair clammed up before finally agreeing that the earring was not their mother's. Taggart also broached the matter of the object in Euphemia's right hand.

'Do you know anything about that?'

Neither Jimmy nor Petrina replied.

'Now listen,' continued Taggart, steadily losing patience, 'if I have to put you and your family in police cells today and tonight, I will do it.'

Jimmy reluctantly broke his silence. 'There was nothing in her hand.'

McVitie had a hunch that the murder was connected with a London jewellery robbery. Three masked raiders had got away with £50,000 from a jeweller's in Shepherd's Bush two days previously. A young police constable had stumbled across the robbery and had been stabbed to death as the men made their escape. The shop assistant had reported that the gang spoke with Scottish accents. The police believed that the raid was linked to a series of similar robberies in south-east England.

Jardine agreed that the same gang could have carried out the other raids. 'Curse of the motorways. They can go down south, commit a job and be back up in five hours.'

Taggart gave him an old-fashioned look. 'When were you last on an English motorway?'

'We'll step up the search for the green car,' said Jardine. 'That's the best clue.'

'I've told the Met,' said McVitie. 'By the way, they're sending up a couple of their guys to liaise with you.'

Taggart surveys the scene of Euphemia Lambie's murder, at the Firhill gypsy site.

'They're what?' said Taggart, dumbfounded.

'One of their policemen was killed,' reasoned McVitie. 'I think they're looking for a little co-operation.'

The Glasgow police gathered vital information about the green car from a local garage, where it had been repaired following the accident. Taggart and Jardine were on their way out when the two Met. detectives arrived.

McVitie attempted to introduce them. 'Jim – I'd like you to meet DCI McGarry and DS Tilling from the Met.'

'Hello,' said Taggart brusquely. 'So – you finally got here.'

'Roadworks on the M1 and M6,' replied McGarry, apologetically.

'We can't stop,' said Taggart.

'We've got a lead on the green car,' added Jardine. 'Belongs to a William Galloway, carpet salesman. We're going to pick him up.'

'We'd better come with you,' suggested McGarry.

'No, you just stay here,' insisted Taggart with mock concern. 'You've had a long, tiring journey. Relax. Have a nice cup of tea. We'll bring him in for you.' At that, they hurried off, leaving McVitie with the open-mouthed Met men.

Taggart and Jardine headed for Kapital Karpets, a Maryhill carpet megastore, where Galloway worked. It was 7.40pm and the store was closed, but Galloway's car was in the otherwise deserted car park. They made for the door, but their progress was halted when a young girl ran out screaming. Her name was Marie. She had found Galloway's body rolled in an offcut of carpet. His neck had been carved up with a lino-cutting knife.

'I take it he didn't do it himself?' said Jardine when Dr Andrews arrived. The pathologist similed. 'Suicides aren't usually that enthusiastic.'

Galloway's superior, Mark Hamilton, a typically thrusting sales executive, revealed that the dead man had been working late to supervise a delivery of vinyl.

'When did you last see him this evening?' queried Jardine.

'About half-past five,' answered Hamilton, momentarily distracted by a magpie flapping about the ceiling of the store. 'I also asked him to get that bird out of here. Before it damaged the stock.'

'It wasn't the bird that did the damage,' said Jardine wryly.

Marie told Taggart all she knew about Billy Galloway. They had a date that night – although their relationship was nothing serious. They just happened to work together. 'I didn't really know him outside this place,' she said, still shaking. 'He's only been up here about nine months. He started with Kapital Karpets down in London, but they move you about to get experience. Can't think why, because every store looks the same.'

Taggart pressed on. 'The mechanic said he found an earring in Galloway's car. Is it yours?'

Marie took a diamond earring out of her bag and handed it to Taggart. 'He said it was one of a pair that he'd bought for me as a present, but I didn't believe him. You can never believe men, can you?'

'I'll need to keep this.'

'One earring's no good to me.'

'Do you know where he was last Monday?'

'His day off. He said he had an accident with the car. Drove it into a wall.'

Everything pointed to Galloway being a member of the gang. The raids took place on his old stamping ground and began six months ago. And they were all staged on Mondays – his regular day off.

The following morning, Taggart and Jardine interviewed all of the carpet store staff in the hope of finding out who Galloway's friends were. Among those questioned was Malcolm Durie, another trainee manager in his mid-twenties. He was addicted to fruit machines. It was an expensive habit. Durie said he knew nothing about Galloway's acquaintances nor where Galloway went last Monday, which also happened to be his day off.

In the meantime, the carpet store was being searched from top to bottom. Eventually, behind a loose wall panel in the loading area of the store, detectives found a replica revolver bearing Galloway's fingerprints, a boiler suit, a ski mask and gloves – but no sign of any jewellery from the London raid.

Taggart had a lot on his plate. McGarry, whose father used to be a detective inspector on Glasgow's South Side but now bred pigs at Torrance, was making snide remarks about the lack of progress in nailing Galloway's accomplices. McGarry himself had left Glasgow some years back for the bright lights of London. That was his stage – not some wintry outpost where time and the police seemed to stand still.

Taggart sought refuge from the tense atmosphere at the station by visiting a riding school for the disabled at which Jean frequently helped out. It was run by a man named Colin Breck, and Taggart had persuaded him to let the Lambies park their caravan on an adjoining field. Taggart was convinced that Jimmy and Petrina were hiding something.

Taggart found Jean immersed in a pile of paperwork in the snack bar area of the school. Pulling up a chair, he sat down next to her. 'I came to check up on those gypsies.'

'You'd hardly know they were here,' she replied. 'They don't say much.'

'They don't trust us, that's why.'

'Can you blame them?' said Jean bluntly. 'You don't exactly have a good record in dealing with them.'

'Don't start …'

'And don't you forget how they were treated by the Nazis.'

This was too much for Taggart to take. 'Jean – I know I'm not an easy man. But you're not comparing me to Hitler!'

The next day, Taggart returned to the carpet store in an attempt to jog Marie's memory about Galloway's associates. The move paid off. She came up with the name of Danny Bonnar, who had once worked at a nearby sandwich bar but was now employed as a chef at a chain of steakhouses called the Trading Post.

Taggart found Bonnar in the kitchen. 'The night before last, between six and eight o'clock. Where were you?'

'I was here. I start at six.'

'Last Monday. All day.'

'That was my day off. Mrs Antrobus was up. She's the owner. She's opening new branches and she asked me to take her round various places.'

'What places?' said Taggart.

'Stirling, Perth, Dundee, St Andrews.'

'Why did she pick you?'

'I don't know. But when you get a hundred quid in your hand, you don't ask questions.'

Taggart decided to check Bonnar's story with Jane Antrobus in person and called at her elegantly furnished flat. She supported Bonnar's alibi to the word

– time, venues, money – and for good measure, it was further corroborated by her companion, casino owner Frank Rourke, a man whom Taggart had once arrested on charges of laundering money. To Taggart's annoyance, the Procurator-Fiscal's office had subsequently dropped the charges against Rourke.

Knowing that the gang would soon try to sell the stolen jewellery, Taggart and Jardine paid a visit to a known fence by the name of George, who ran a clock and repair shop in the city. At first, he denied all knowledge, but later that day, tempted by the £5,000 reward, he anonymously phoned New Scotland Yard, telling them that he had information about the murder of the London policeman. However, he stipulated that he would only deal with the Met. He had helped Taggart in the past and, as he put it, had been 'shat on from a great height'.

To Taggart's annoyance, both Jane Antrobus and her lover, Frank Rourke, corroborate Danny Bonnar's alibi during the murders.

The message was relayed to McGarry, who decided that he and Tilling should act independently of the Glasgow boys. When Taggart found out, he was predictably furious, especially since the arranged rendezvous had fallen through. From the description of the caller's voice – a Geordie accent with a stutter – Taggart immediately knew it was George. He and Jardine sped to George's shop. There they found the closed sign up and George's blood-soaked body lying in the back room. His throat had been cut.

Acting on Taggart's feeling that the gypsies were keeping something back, Jardine endeavoured to befriend the pretty but vulnerable Petrina. They chatted, to little effect, until suddenly the door to the caravan burst open. Brother Jimmy was brandishing a knife.

'What are you doing in there?' he demanded.

Jardine kept his cool. 'You can cut yourself on one of those.'

Ironically, the incident worked in Taggart's favour. For it was the threat of charging Jimmy with assaulting an officer that finally made Petrina reveal what had been in her mother's hand at the time of the murder. She had been clutching two pieces of wood and a black feather, to act as a curse on her killers.

Taggart rounded on Jimmy. 'Look, I want the two bits of wood and the black feather that you took out of your mother's hand.'

Jimmy stared at the ground with a sullen expression.

'Look at me and not your shoes!' bawled Taggart. 'Or I'll have you for tampering with evidence.'

Slowly, Jimmy reached in his pocket and pulled out the feather with the pieces of wood laid in a V across the top. He held it in a manner which made Taggart think he was putting the curse on him. For a moment Taggart hesitated, but then snatched the items from Jimmy. The feather was that of a magpie.

As Taggart and McVitie discussed the gypsy curse, Jardine hurried in to announce that fingerprints found at the clock shop tallied with those taken from Malcolm Durie at Kapital Karpets. Taggart was just on his way out when the phone rang. Jean's invalid car had been involved in a road accident. She was lying in a coma in the intensive care unit of the Western Infirmary.

While Taggart sat at Jean's bedside day and night, another corpse turned up. It was that of Malcolm Durie, stabbed in the neck on a deserted building site at night. Durie had clearly been one of Galloway's accomplices. He had been overlooked because his alibi for the Monday of the robbery and the murder of Euphemia Lambie seemed to check out and, like Galloway, he had no previous form.

Jardine turned to McVitie. 'You'll think this is silly, sir.'

'Try me.'

'The gypsy woman puts a curse on her three killers. Just a magpie feather and two pieces of wood. Now two of them are dead.'

'I hope you're not trying to tell me you believe in it?' said a sceptical McVitie.

'When Jimmy Lambie gave us the feather and pieces of wood, he held them in his hand ... like that.'

'Go on.'

'He was putting a curse on Jim, sir. That was yesterday. Just a few hours before the accident.'

McVitie remained unimpressed. 'A detective needs imagination – but not too much.'

There seemed to be a clue to Durie's killer – a wallet found in his pocket. It belonged to a Derek Paisley. Traced to the amusement arcade, Paisley insisted that Durie had lifted his wallet while he was playing the machines. He also mentioned that Durie had been trying to sell him a ring. 'He had a handful of them. Big silver jobs. I told him I didn't want one.'

Curiously, Durie's own wallet, which he always carried about with him, was nowhere to be found.

Paisley's story held firm and Jardine had no option but to let him go. McGarry and Tilling stormed off in protest. The rift between the two forces was widening by the minute.

At the hospital, where Taggart had somehow persuaded the sister, against her better judgement, to provide him with an office, Jardine reported on the latest developments.

'Perfect cover,' mused Taggart. 'Two guys in respectable white-collar jobs. No previous. In need of a bit of excitement … Suppose the third is, too.'

'Wouldn't they need a pro?' said Jardine.

'No professional would take a pair like Galloway and Durie with him! That's the trap we're falling into. These guys are lucky amateurs.'

Just then, a constable arrived with a pile of files.

'What about the press?' asked Jardine.

'Let them think it's a homicidal maniac' replied Taggart, mischievously, 'with a bent for carpet salesmen!'

Aware that the carpet store manager also had Mondays off, Taggart instructed Jardine to reinterview Mark Hamilton, who was fretting about the effect the murders were having on staff morale. It was soon abundantly clear that he would no more associate with the likes of Galloway and Durie than take five minutes extra for lunch. However, in the course of their conversation, Marie produced a postcard which had just arrived for Durie. It read: '*M – off to Marseilles. hope to shed a few stones in weight, as before. will meet up with some new freinds.*' Jardine immediately noted the misspelling of 'friends'.

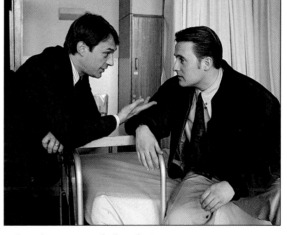

When the postcard message was relayed to Taggart, his thoughts turned to Danny Bonnar. 'I'd like to put a tail on our friend Bonnar. Maybe I was too quick to believe his alibi witnesses. They both have lots of foreign connections.'

Jardine and Tilling followed Bonnar and Mrs Antrobus to a multi-storey car park where, hindered by a decoy driver planted by Rourke, they succeeded in losing them. The blow to the investigation was bad enough but nowhere near as traumatic as having to report the news to Taggart. They found him in the intensive care unit, conducting his vigil.

'What do you mean, you lost them?' shrieked Taggart.

'They went into a multi-storey car park,' mumbled Jardine.

'I don't care how it happened! Two experienced detectives do a job like a pair of five-year-olds out of cadet school. Do I have to leave Jean's bedside and do everything myself?'

Jardine tried to appease him. 'We've got the car under surveillance. And

DCI McGarry and DC Tilling from the Met. turn out to be even more involved in the case than Taggart imagined.

both their places are being watched as well.'

The nurse attending to the drip in Jean's arm suddenly noticed a flicker in Jean's eyes. Oblivious to this, Taggart continued ranting at Jardine and Tilling. 'And in the meantime? Suppose they go somewhere, do something, where are we? And how the hell did you lose them in a car park?'

'Your man was driving,' said Tilling. 'A car got in front of him.'

'And what did you do?' boomed Taggart. 'Radio for assistance? No! You decide to play at Cagney and Lacey. I'd have done better with a couple of women.'

Hearing the commotion, the sister marched in. But before she could berate Taggart, the nurse excitedly drew his attention to Jean.

'Mr Taggart. Your wife.'

Taggart rushed to her bedside. Her eyes and lips were moving. He held her hand tenderly and was able to feel movement in her fingers.

'Jean, talk to me. It's me. Jim.' The nurse encouraged him to continue. 'Look at me, Jean.'

Jean looked up and whispered weakly: 'What's the shouting …?'

The familiar sound of Taggart's temper had brought her out of the coma.

Jardine managed to salvage something from the car-park fiasco by breaking into the car abandoned there by Bonnar and Mrs Antrobus. On the floor of the car, he found Bonnar's bank-book. The bank manager told Jardine and Tilling that Bonnar and a woman answering to the description of Jane Antrobus had been in about an hour earlier. Bonnar had wanted access to his deed box. With Jean now recovering rapidly, Taggart was back on the case full time, and his first task was to join in the ceremonial opening of Bonnar's deed-box. It was empty, apart from a cassette tape.

Convinced that the cassette would provide them with the lead they had been waiting for, McVitie, Taggart, Jardine, McGarry and Tilling stood in hushed expectation to listen to its contents. Instead of bearing vital evidence, they were treated to the sounds of Danny Bonnar and Jane Antrobus making love …

Frustrated, Taggart decided to lean on Frank Rourke at his casino. Rourke protested that he knew nothing of Mrs Antrobus's movements – in or out of bed – theirs was just a business relationship, he said. But when Cook, his henchman, walked in, Jardine recognized him as the man who had helped Antrobus and Bonnar escape at the multi-storey.

'Look, I was doing the lady a favour, that's all,' insisted Rourke, realizing that he was cornered.

Taggart was in no mood for being fobbed off. 'You do me a favour, Rourke. Or by this time next year, this place'll be a supermarket! Now, where are they?'

'I've no idea.'

'Do better.'

'That's the truth. I lent Jane a car, that's all.'

'Make and type.'

'A Roller. Registration number BET 521.'

While the hunt was on for the car, Taggart visited Jean in hospital. He was putting out some of the many cards she had received from well-wishers when he accidentally knocked a small gift card to the floor. It had come with some flowers sent by McGarry. Taggart opened the envelope and read the message. It said: '*To Mrs. Taggart, from Andy McGarry and David Tilling (your husband's freinds from the Met)*'

Taggart stared at the message intently. Something about it troubled him – it was the misspelling of the word 'friend'. He went over to his file, plucked out a photocopy of the postcard message sent to Malcolm Durie and compared the spelling and the handwriting. As he ran his eyes from one to the other, the truth dawned. McGarry had sent the postcard to put them on a false trail.

It was McGarry and Tilling who had masterminded the jewellery robberies carried out by Galloway, Durie and Bonnar. They had caught Galloway on his first job and had made him an offer he couldn't refuse. But now that Bonnar had stabbed the London policeman as well as Euphemia Lambie, the situation had got out of control. McGarry had silenced Galloway and Durie, as well as George, the fence. Only Bonnar remained a threat. McGarry was desperate to get his hands on an incriminating cassette tape made by Bonnar of their first meeting. To deliver the tape and Bonnar, McGarry had recruited the services of Jane Antrobus. She in turn owed McGarry a favour after he had once tipped off her criminal husband, thereby allowing him to flee to Marbella before he could be arrested. It was she who had switched the tapes in Bonnar's deed-box.

Bonnar thought he was chauffeuring Mrs Antrobus to Spain, but that night she made him stop off at McGarry senior's pig farm. She said she had something to drop off there. The old man was out for the evening, but waiting for her were McGarry and Tilling. She handed over the tape. McGarry eagerly pushed it into his father's player.

Galloway's voice was heard, saying: 'This is Danny, this is Malcolm, they're both clean. Malcolm works beside me. Danny used to …'

McGarry: 'You all know what's expected?'

Bonnar: 'Billy told us …'

McGarry: 'Right, listen. We're not talking peanuts here. None of you guys are known, except by us. You're all in regular jobs. You're 400 miles away. None of you will be suspected. We'll give you the jobs to do, we'll tell you when.'

Bonnar: 'If we get caught, do you get us off?'

Tilling: 'You don't get caught.'

McGarry: 'We can create diversions. There's money for all of us.'

The tape ended. McGarry switched off the machine with satisfaction.

The pieces finally begin to fit together for Taggart.

'Debt repaid?' said Jane Antrobus.

'Repaid in full,' nodded McGarry.

Outside in the car, Bonnar was growing impatient. He strolled over to the house and, through a gap in the curtains, recognized McGarry talking to Mrs Antrobus. He had seen him before with Taggart.

Realizing he had been tricked, Bonnar ran back to the car and started the engine. Hearing the noise, McGarry snatched up a shotgun, raced out into the courtyard and fired at the windscreen. In his panic to escape, Bonnar reversed into the swill bins and stalled the car. McGarry hauled him out.

Wounded and bleeding, Bonnar screamed at Mrs Antrobus. 'What have you done! They'll kill me! Like they killed the others!'

McGarry was hell bent on further destruction and, depositing the shotgun by the side of a pen, dragged Bonnar over to the food shed. He held Bonnar's head into the feeder. After all, pigs will eat anything. But Jane Antrobus wanted no part of murder. She knew nothing about any of the killings. She snatched up the abandoned shotgun. Nervously, she pointed it at McGarry.

'Let him go,' she yelled. 'He's had enough!'

'Put down the gun,' ordered McGarry. 'Dave – take it off her.'

Tilling had also had enough. 'Let's just get out of here, Andy.'

McGarry would not listen. 'Give me the gun, Jane. He's a cop killer. Or maybe that's the type you like sleeping with.'

He advanced on her, menacingly, knowing she would drop the gun when he got close. After all, she was just a woman. She had never held a shotgun before. She couldn't even hold it steady. Nearer and nearer he came, until he was within grabbing range. Jane Antrobus was petrified. He lunged for the gun. The shock made her pull the trigger. It went off, sending him reeling backwards.

Just then, Taggart and Jardine roared up. Mrs Antrobus dropped the gun. With McGarry and Bonnar lying wounded, Jardine cornered Tilling.

'McGarry killed them, not me,' pleaded Tilling. 'The fence, too.'

It cut no ice with Taggart. 'It's a pity for you he didn't finish his education up here. He might have learned to spell.'

ROGUES' GALLERY

It was one of Jardine's more pleasurable assignments – a visit from a cool blonde reporting the theft of a dark green Citroen. As a rule, such matters would have been dealt with by uniform, but there had been a spate of stolen executive cars in the city just lately and so Valerie Sinclair fell into the lap of CID. Jardine was instantly smitten. For Miss Sinclair made a refreshing change from the usual diet of drunks, dossers and weirdos who entered the portals of Maryhill. So, bypassing the painters who were redecorating the office, he put on his best smile and nervously wiped from his hand the residue of the machine tea he had just been drinking. He did not wish his air of sophistication to be wrecked during their very first exchange.

For the interview, he was thoroughness personified, copiously taking down notes as if she were revealing the true identity of Jack the Ripper.

'What model?', began Jardine, almost relieved that the desk between them stopped him staring at her legs.

'God, I haven't a clue … It's not my car … belongs to the boss.'

'And his name?'

'Gallagher … Neil Gallagher.' Ruefully, she added: 'I was running an errand for him at the time.'

'Well,' said Jardine reassuringly, 'we'll soon check up and get the model from DVLC.' He had reached the interesting point. 'Do you have a contact address?'

'Fourteen … er, no, the best thing would be the gallery. I'm opening a new art gallery in Canal Street for Mr Gallagher. Here's my card.'

Jardine read the card aloud. 'The Canal Gallery … Artistic Director.' Brains and beauty. He was suitably impressed.

Within two days, the feeling was mutual. The car had been found in one piece. Jardine seized the opportunity to tell Miss Sinclair the good news in person.

Vallerie from the gallery.

**Transmission date:
31 December 1990**
Writer: Stuart Hepburn
Producer: Robert Love
Director: Alan Macmillan

SUPPORTING CAST:
DET. CON. JACKIE REID
– Blythe Duff
VALERIE SINCLAIR
– Edita Brychta
NEIL GALLAGHER
– Jack Galloway
SCOTT KERR
– Ross Dunsmore
PETER LATIMER
– Peter Mullan

Jardine and
Taggart brush up
on their art.

He strode into the Canal Gallery, housed in a converted warehouse overlooking the Clyde, in the middle of the opening exhibition – the work of a young Glasgow artist, Scott Kerr. With his Doc Martens, shaven head, ill-fitting secondhand suit and roll-your-own cigarettes, Kerr was strangely at odds with the general air of arty small talk, house wine and prawn vol-au-vents.

Jardine made straight for Valerie Sinclair, handing her a pair of shoes recovered from the vehicle.

'You've found it?' she asked hopefully, spying the shoes.

'Lying with an empty petrol tank in Bishopbriggs. New ignition switch and it'll be none the worse.'

'Thanks for your hard work. Mind you, it was only leased, I discovered. I'll tell Mr Gallagher.'

Her eyes steered Jardine towards the figure of Neil Gallagher, who was busily chatting on a mobile phone. Gallagher was in his late thirties, fashionably dressed, a working-class boy made good. He had also worked hard at his tan.

While an ageing jazz band played a laid-back version of 'Georgia', Jardine engaged Valerie in artistic discussion. Suddenly, the jaws of the assembled throng dropped in unison at the arrival of a noisy protest group from the Barrfoot Community Arts Centre, led by Peter Latimer, a hard, muscular man of around thirty-eight. They proceeded to thrust leaflets into unwilling hands, promoting the 'Great Barrfoot People's Art Show'.

'What's all this?' whispered Jardine.

'Latimer asked us to exhibit some community art work,' replied Valerie. 'Mr Gallagher deemed it "unsuitable".'

Witnessing the disintegration of his launch, Gallagher ordered the gallery security guard, Jack Greig, to evict Latimer and his cohorts.

Latimer pushed Greig away and, in the process, almost succeeded in wrecking a wood and metal sculpture. Gallagher's fury erupted. In an instant, the businessman veneer vanished. He had relapsed to his street-fighting days.

'I'm going to have you, Latimer.'

'Temper, temper,' sneered Latimer.

Screaming 'Bastard!', Gallagher lunged at his antagonist, but Scott Kerr held him back.

At that point, Jardine deemed it wise to intervene. 'Excuse me, gents. I think we should all just cool down.' He turned to Latimer. 'You've made your point. Just leave.'

'Who rattled your cage?' snarled Latimer.

Jardine produced his warrant card. Sensing that discretion was the better part of valour, Latimer smiled and put his hands up. 'I'm going, I'm going.'

Still red-faced, Gallagher did his best to compose himself. 'Hey, come on, everyone, the party's just beginning. Play something.'

Even the band were too shocked by Gallagher's personality swing to respond immediately.

'Play!' he repeated, more forcefully than before.

This time, they broke into a rendition of 'Misty'. Faces gradually stopped looking at feet and a sense of normality returned. Jardine, too, prepared to leave. As he did so, he handed Valerie his card.

'This is my number at the station. If you ever need any … help … in the future, give me a ring.'

'What sort of help?'

'Oh, I can turn my hand to most things. See you.'

Back at the station, Jardine bumped into Taggart, who was supposed to be having three days off to do some gardening. It was hard enough to get Taggart to take time off anyway, but now this break had been rudely interrupted by the discovery of a body at a car breaker's yard. It had been in the boot of a white Cortina, but had only been spotted by the operators after it had gone through the crusher.

By the time Taggart and Jardine arrived, the area had been cordoned off and a green tent erected. Dr Andrews was waiting for them. They entered the tent. Inside, on a couple of trestle tables lay six sausages of metal, from which blood had oozed profusely. Jardine had to look away. Taggart was made of sterner stuff.

'Got a tin opener?'

The crane operator, Norrie Walker, was an enthusiastic interviewee. 'I'd say he was killed first, then dumped in the boot,' he pronounced, rubbing the dust from his hands. 'I seen his wrists, all tied up. Well, I think they were his wrists.'

'Yes, but how did you find him?' asked Taggart.

'A bit cut up … Got a dog once, but never a human. We just found a bullet too. Nine mill.'

'What do you know about bullets?' said Taggart, condescendingly.

'I was in the TA. Gangland slaying, if you ask me.'

'I get paid for the theories, Mr Walker. Just tell me what you know.'

'Ah well, like I says to the polis, if I hadnae noticed him in the boot, he'd have ended up a set of cutlery.'

Dr Andrews set up a temporary forensic laboratory in the police garage, where he and his team attempted to reconstruct the position of the body in the boot from the state of the dead man's clothes.

'It was like reconstituting sliced sausage,' said Dr Andrews in his matter-of-fact way.

'What can you tell us?' said Taggart.

'We reckon he was bound and got a bullet to the head.'

'So the guy at the scrapyard was right,' muttered Jardine, a shade peeved at the success of an amateur detective.

It emerged that the Cortina had been stolen from a car park in Barrfoot three days earlier. It belonged to a sixty-five-year-old retired nurse, who insisted that the boot was empty when the car went missing.

Taggart examined a length of blue polypropylene tape, found with the body. 'This means that they supplied the stuff they tied him up with.'

'It's newspaper binding, isn't it?' said Dr Andrews.

'Mike's just going to check up on it.'

The most important find at the breaker's yard was a finger, belonging to the deceased. A print taken from it revealed its erstwhile owner to be twenty-two-year-old Thomas James Wilson from Notting Hill. He had form for shoplifting, vagrancy and two counts of possession. About what was left of his person, they found two grammes of heroin and a return ticket to Euston. He had travelled up to Glasgow three days previously.

'So why does someone want to kill a small-time junkie?' pondered McVitie.

'Could have been a courier,' answered Taggart.

'And somebody relieved him of his goods. Better check with the Drugs Squad. Any large deals on the go?'

'I've done it. Not a thing. If he *was* on a drugs carry, it'd have to be a big one to make it worth killing him for. At least we've got a bullet. Your average drugs ned tends to favour a shotgun through the teeth.'

Ballistics identified the bullet as having come from a nine millimetre automatic, possibly a Browning or a Luger. Jardine had confirmed that the polypropylene tape was commonly used for wrapping bundles of newspapers, but Detective Constable Jackie Reid, newly assigned to CID aid, had a theory of her own. She thought the tape might have been slipped through the window to assist in the stealing of the Cortina. Taggart was very nearly impressed.

His sources on the streets threw up the name of Flash Frankie McGovern. The word was that McGovern was setting up a big deal in Barrfoot. Meanwhile, through his blossoming relationship with Valerie Sinclair, at whose house he spent the night, Jardine learned that the Barrfoot Community Centre had mysteriously burnt down and that Latimer, believing Gallagher to be responsible, had turned up at the gallery in threatening mood. Fortunately, Gallagher was away on business for the day. Jardine decided to keep the information to himself.

Gallagher's respite was short-lived, however, for the following morning, his body was found in the boot of a car in the same breaker's yard. He was lying in roughly the same position as Wilson and had also been shot through the head. The only difference was that this time Norrie Walker spotted the corpse before it was crushed. Taggart sifted through Gallagher's pockets and brought out a small packet of cocaine.

At the Canal Gallery, Taggart fired a couple of routine questions at Greig, the security guard.

'You locked up last night?'

'Yes, sir. Mr Gallagher left a message that he'd be coming back later, but I never saw him.'

'Worked here long, Mr Greig?'

'Two months. I don't know what's going to happen now, though.'

Taggart pointed to a pile of debris on the floor. 'What's all this?'

'We'd a small incident yesterday.'

'Involving Gallagher?'

'Indirectly. A gentleman smashed the sculpture. I did report it to the police, but no one came down.'

'And who was this gentleman?'

'His name's Peter Latimer, sir.'

'Peter Latimer? The ex-lifer?'

'I think your colleague met him,' said Greig.

Jardine looked sheepish – as well he might. Taggart tore a strip off him in the privacy of the gallery office.

'Latimer's done time for murder, he comes here and threatens Gallagher, and you didn't think it was important?'

'I never connected it, sir,' said Jardine, apologetically.

'You never connected it? Mike, there's a nutter going round Glasgow pumping bullets into folk and locking them in car boots. I don't want to give him the chance to do a third one. What's wrong with you? Are you on heat or something?'

Little did Taggart know, but that was a little too close to the mark.

Unaware of Jardine's involvement with the lady, Taggart quizzed Valerie Sinclair, who revealed that Gallagher had cash-flow problems.

'But there are "sold" stickers on all these paintings,' said Taggart, puzzled.

'Mr Gallagher said he was meeting a client yesterday,' replied Valerie. 'Brought him in here after we closed for a private viewing. My presence was not required.'

'Did that surprise you?'

'The deal? It can happen. A dealer sees an outstanding talent and moves in quick. Mr Gallagher spent the last five years in the States. I presume he has contacts.'

'And where did you work before you came here?'

'A private gallery in London. Before that I worked in Berlin.'

Taggart's mind immediately linked to the Luger. 'Berlin? You don't own a gun by any chance?'

Valerie was taken aback. 'No, no, I don't.'

Taggart made for the exit. 'Oh, by the way, where were you yesterday evening?'

'At home. Curled up with a detective novel.'

Neither Latimer nor Scott Kerr, who was owed money by Gallagher, were particularly forthcoming although Kerr did admit to having been angry after finding out that Gallagher had 'exclusively contracted' him to a company in Boston, Massachusetts, which he'd never heard of.

Taggart decided to have Latimer's flat searched. Beneath the bed, Jardine found a length of blue polypropylene tape. Excitedly, he reported the find to Taggart.

'And get this. Turns out Latimer was in charge of a day centre that got closed down because one of his colleagues got caught dealing smack … Flash McGovern.'

Taggart tightened his lips in delight. 'We've got him.'

But he was a trifle premature. Latimer's lawyer, Ian McKenzie, was making loud noises about the fact that his client was still being detained yet had not been charged. With insufficient evidence, McVitie had no option but to order Latimer's release. Taggart was not a happy man.

It was Jardine's turn to feel perplexed when Reid discovered that the gallery was registered in the name of Valerie Sinclair, a move taken because Gallagher had been declared bankrupt five years earlier.

'He was claiming VAT on paintings,' said Reid. 'Pretending to export them, then getting rid of them here.'

'I want to know whose paintings were involved in the con,' demanded Taggart.

His next port of call was Valerie Sinclair. He found that her departure from the Glass Gallery in Berlin had been less than amicable. But there was more. He met up with Jardine, who was watching Latimer's flat.

'She'd been having an affair with Gallagher,' declared Taggart.

The colour drained from Jardine's face. 'What?'

'But they fell out over another woman last week. What do you make of that?'

Jardine was speechless.

Taggart wasn't. 'I think our Valerie from the gallery is up to her pretty little neck in this.'

Just when Taggart was about to increase the pressure on Latimer and Valerie Sinclair, the discovery of the bodies of two local heavies in a derelict flat seemed to bring the case to a satisfactory conclusion. The presence in the flat of a Luger, £1,000 in cash, a discarded syringe and a stash of heroin appeared to point to the fact that these two had murdered Wilson and Gallagher before accidentally overdosing on pure heroin. It called for a celebration in the pub. The party was in full swing when Taggart came off the phone after talking to Dr Andrews.

'Good news, sir?' asked Reid.

'That heroin was the purest stuff the labs have ever seen,' confirmed Taggart. 'The junkies *did* die of an overdose.'

Jardine raised his glass of mineral water. 'Here's to crime …'

Taggart had not finished. '… Two days before Gallagher was shot.'

The party was well and truly pooped.

Next day was Sunday. But it was no day of rest for Taggart and his team. Taggart had a new theory – that the murders of Wilson and Gallagher were not linked after all. Wilson was indeed murdered by the two junkies – he was a courier, ripped off over a heroin deal. 'But,' proposed Taggart, 'let's say you wanted to murder Gallagher *and* get away with it. You wait for a suitable, unsolved murder to take place, then you kill him in exactly the same way.'

'But how could anyone have duplicated the murder so well?' mused McVitie. 'We didn't release the information. Who had access to the details?'

Taggart suspected that the enthusiastic Norrie Walker might have inadvertently leaked them.

'Did you tell anyone, and I mean anyone, about what you saw in the tent that day?'

'You told me not to,' declared Walker. 'I never even told the wife.'

'Are you sure?'

'Of course …'

Taggart resigned himself to not getting any

Taggart tries out his theory of Gallagher's murder on McVitie.

further and was about to leave when Walker called him back.

'Oh no, I tell a lie. I told the boy's father.'

'His father?' repeated Taggart.

'He came to see me at the yard,' explained Walker. 'He said his wife couldn't rest till they found out what happened to him. How he died, like.'

Taggart was mystified. 'Wilson never had a father. He was an orphan.'

Before he could get a proper description of the 'father', Taggart was interrupted by Reid. Her Customs and Excise inquiries had come up with the name and address of the artist whose paintings Gallagher had been exporting five years earlier. They sped round to a house in Maryhill owned by a Mrs Sheila Ross. She had a son of about twenty-five, David, who was in a wheelchair and who seemed to hear or understand very little.

Meanwhile, Jardine wanted a few answers from Valerie Sinclair. He arrived at the gallery to be told by Jack Greig that Valerie had gone to the airport with some paintings. Jardine rushed back outside in time to see his car being driven away by joyriders. He commandeered Greig's car and the pair headed for the airport.

Back at the Rosses', Sheila showed Taggart a portfolio of beautiful pencil drawings that her son had drawn to get into art school. 'He got the Rome Scholarship, you know. But he decided to stay here. Signed the contract for

Mr Gallagher, you see. Promised the world … turned out it bound him hand and foot. When the paintings were sent away, he got so depressed. Went out in his Dad's car one night and got drunk. Smashed it up.' She gently stroked David's forehead. 'Lucky to be alive really.'

Taggart continued to leaf disinterestedly through the drawings until he suddenly came across one of a person he recognized only too well. It was of David's father – except that Taggart knew him better as gallery security man Jack Greig.

'I'm afraid he took the accident awful badly,' sighed Sheila Ross. 'He's been troubled with his nerves ever since.'

'Could we have a word with him?' said Taggart.

'Well, no. He's at work. He's a car park attendant.'

'On a Sunday?'

Taggart and Reid hurried to the gallery, where they learned that Jardine and Greig had set off for the airport.

'Call the airport,' barked Taggart. 'Get the plane stopped.'

'Which plane?' asked Reid innocently.

'Every bloody plane.'

Thanks to Taggart's delaying tactics, the entire population of Glasgow

Jack Greig makes a point to Jardine.

seemed to be on the airport concourse, including Valerie Sinclair, with the paintings which she had, in fact, sold perfectly legitimately. The only people who weren't present were Jardine and Greig.

Jardine was driving towards the airport when a lorry blocked the road.

'Turn left,' shouted Greig. 'I know a short cut.'

As he followed Greig's directions through the streets, Jardine became puzzled.

'This doesn't go to the airport.'

'We're not going to the airport,' said Greig coldly.

Jardine turned to his passenger for an explanation but instead found a nine millimetre Browning pointed at his temple. It dawned on him that Greig was the killer.

Greig forced him to drive to Maryhill police station. 'I'm going to get it all off my chest,' he announced, a manic grin spreading across his face. He was completely mad.

The Desk Sergeant stopped mid-sentence as Greig, still smiling, pushed an ashen-faced Jardine through the main office at gunpoint.

Jardine tried to exert an aura of calmness. 'Mr Ross wants to make a statement. I'm just going to take him into the office.'

In Taggart's office, Greig made Jardine sit down and write. Greig was becoming increasingly agitated and clasped the gun two-handed, pointing it directly at Jardine, who was doing his best to take down the words.

'Five years isn't long to wait,' blurted Greig, 'not when your son has a life sentence. In some ways death's a release …'

His finger tightened around the trigger.

'… A blessed release. I released Gallagher from his guilt. And now I can release us too.'

Beads of perspiration ran down Jardine's cheek.

At that point, McVitie, blissfully unaware of what was going on around him, sauntered out of his office ready for a game of golf and stumbled across the hostage scene.

McVitie's unexpected entry distracted Greig, enabling Jardine to make a lunge for him. There was a loud bang and a streak of red smeared across the glass of the door. It was red paint, left behind by the men redecorating the station. While a relieved and thankful Jardine sat motionless holding the gun, Greig lay slumped across the table, sobbing: 'My wee boy … he took my wee boy.'

If nothing else, it would give McVitie something to talk about in the clubhouse.

VIOLENT DELIGHTS

Taggart surveyed the scene wearily. It was too early in the morning for mysterious deaths. The previous night, when Taggart had been working late at the office, a car had veered off a country road on the outskirts of Glasgow, careered down a steep slope, ploughed into a tree and burst into flames. Inside lay the body of a young man. Now, at a time of day when most civilized people were still having breakfast, Taggart, Jardine and Reid found themselves standing at the foot of the slope, looking at a burnt-out car and a partially charred tree.

Jardine offered a crumb of comfort. 'Registration number belongs to an Alexander Telfer, 5 Doggetts Road, Anniesland.'

Taggart stroked his chin, thoughtfully. 'Nobody reports the accident. Nobody sees the fire.'

'Not many people use this road at night, sir.' said Jardine, trying to be helpful.

'What was he doing on it?' snapped Taggart.

'Well …'

Reid attempted to come to Jardine's rescue. 'There's no information as yet. His wife's in hospital. She was supposed to have been with him last night.'

'What's wrong with her?' demanded Taggart, his voice utterly bereft of sympathy.

Transmission date:
1 January 1992
Writer: Glenn Chandler
Producer: Robert Love
Director: Alan Macmillan

SUPPORTING CAST:
PHILIP DEMPSTER – Tom Smith
FRANÇOISE CAMPBELL – Florence Guérin
ANDY COLLINS – John Dougall
TONY JACOVELLI – Paul Hickey
IAN MCLAUGHLIN – Jason Hetherington
SHEILA MCINTOSH – Natalie Robb
ANGUS COLLINS – Ronald Fraser
MICK DAWSON – Alastair Cording
AUNTY HETTIE – Sheila Donald
PETER CAMPBELL – Ronald Aitken
ALEC TELFER – Hugh Larkin

Jardine and Taggart ponder Alec Telfer's death.

'Maternity,' continued Reid. 'She gave birth to a six-and-a-half pound baby boy at 8.05pm.'

Taggart shook his head in despair. 'Have you got any useful facts?'

Jardine and Reid exchanged awkward glances. It was clear they hadn't.

Neither was Dr Andrews able to offer much assistance at that stage. 'He wasn't belted in,' proclaimed the pathologist. 'Whether he was dead or unconscious when the fire started, I won't be able to tell you till I get the body back.'

Before quitting the scene, Taggart decided to take one further look at the car. Suddenly he spotted something shining on the floor. He bent down. It was a keyring in the shape of a small silver fox. It had been blackened by the heat of the fire. Carefully, he lifted it up to read the lettering. The writing was in French, a language as foreign to Taggart as English.

The inscription read: *Nous sommes dans toutes les voitures.* Jardine and Reid translated it as: 'We are in every car.'

Encouraged by the find, however meaningless it seemed, Taggart took a closer look at what was left of the car interior. He sat in the remains of the driving seat, looking in the rear-view mirror back up the hill to the road. He was uneasy about the whole business. It seemed too neat. He noticed the remnants of a whisky bottle in the front passenger well, then tried the gear-stick. It moved freely in the gear-box. His suspicions were confirmed.

He turned to Jardine. 'How could it run off the road in neutral?'

Jardine and Reid visited Telfer's wife, Marilyn, in hospital.

'I knew it would happen one day,' she said tenderly holding the new-born baby.

'Knew what would happen, Mrs Telfer?' queried Reid.

'He'd kill himself. Driving. He would drink. Always saying – it wouldn't happen to him.

'Did he have any reason to be on the Coatbridge road last night?'

'No. Why? That isn't even on his way home.'

'It's where his car was found,' explained Jardine.

'What was he doing there?,' wondered Mrs Telfer. 'He knew our baby was due any day …'

'Where did he work?'

'Collins and Son in Maryhill. He was an undertaker.'

Taggart was familiar with the firm, an old established one run by Angus Collins and his son Andy. As Taggart and Jardine arrived there, Andy Collins, a young man of thirty with an air of sympathetic efficiency, was guiding a group of mourners out of the chapel. He broke away to come over and talk to

Taggart. Dental records had confirmed the body to be that of Alec Telfer. Taggart broke the news to Andy Collins.

'Oh my God,' said Andy, shocked. He quickly recovered the composure which went with the job. 'How did it happen? Was it a car accident?'

'What makes you say that?' asked Taggart, suspiciously.

'My father will explain. He was a silly boy, Mr Taggart.' Andy discreetly tipped his hand to his mouth to convey the message before returning to the funeral party.

Taggart and Jardine found old Angus Collins in a yard surrounded by dozens of coffins. Jardine looked distinctly uneasy in such a sinister setting.

'I thought you were retiring,' said Taggart.

'No, no. Still keeping my hand in,' replied Angus. 'And keeping an eye on Andy. You know what these young ones are like. They want to change everything for the sake of change.'

'How do you change an undertakers?' whispered Jardine to Taggart.

'Funeral directors, if you don't mind, son,' corrected Angus. 'It's quite easy. You just move to bigger, more comfortable premises and people forget you're the same firm. Andy went to the States, saw a lot of funeral parlours there. Funfairs I call them.'

Angus Collins, Alec Telfer's employer at the undertakers, fills in some details about the murder victim.

Taggart relayed the demise of Alec Telfer.

'Well, he'd been with us for two weeks and I doubt he'd still have been with us after another two,' declared Angus. 'He wasn't cut out for the job. You see, what happens sometimes is they have no problem driving the car or dealing with the bereaved. But they just can't handle the remains – touch the dead. You know what it's like, Jim. We put up a shield. We have to. It's part of the job. But Alec just wasn't getting used to it at all.'

Jardine understood only too well. 'Did it drive him to drink?'

'Not on the job – or he'd have been out the same day,' answered Angus firmly. 'But I hear he was in the habit of taking a few before he drove home.'

Taggart produced the keyring in a transparent plastic bag. The key was still attached.

'Have you ever seen that key or the ring?'

'I know every key to this building,' said Angus, studying it closely. 'And this isn't one of them.' His thoughts turned to business. 'I'd better get on to his wife and offer to handle the funeral.'

Cause of death was given as shock from burns. The presence of carbon monoxide in Telfer's body fluids indicated that he had died after the fire had started. The blood alcohol level was 390 milligrams, equivalent to nearly eleven pints of beer or two-thirds of a bottle of whisky – in other words, almost total stupor.

Jardine was disappointed. 'Could he have been knocked unconscious?'

'No evidence of it,' said Dr Andrews. 'What's your theory?'

'Somebody got him drunk and pushed his car off the road, forgetting that cars don't crash in neutral.'

Even though none of the staff at the funeral premises recognized it, the silver fox keyring still appeared to be the best clue, especially when Marilyn Telfer categorically stated that it did not belong to her late husband. She also insisted that, although he enjoyed a drink, he never drank at the wheel of a car. Enquiries revealed that the keyring was produced by Compagnie Renard SA in Lille, *renard* being French for fox. It was purely a promotional item and would not have been on sale in Glasgow.

Taggart found himself involved in more dealing with Collins and Son when Jean's Aunty Hettie, by no means Taggart's favourite relative, died from a stroke. Knowing how fond Jean was of the old girl, Taggart swapped the coffin she had chosen for a more expensive model. The gesture was not well received.

'She never wanted a lot of fuss made about her funeral,' said Jean frostily at the viewing room. 'A plain elm one would have done. This is solid oak!'

'Well, she doesn't have to know,' protested Taggart. 'I did it for *you*.'

His apology had just about been accepted when he compounded his sins in the limousine on the way to the funeral. Gazing ahead, he spotted that the same Renard keyring was hanging from the key in the ignition.

'Stop the car!' yelled Taggart.

'What?' said the stunned driver.

'Where did you get that keyring?' barked Taggart.

Jean could not believe her ears. 'Jim!'

'Jean, do you mind, this is important,' implying that Aunty Hettie's funeral was anything but.

'Mick Dawson gave it to me,' answered the driver. 'He's with the hearse. Did you really want me to stop?'

Before he could reply, Jean laid down the law. 'Jim, if you hold up Aunty Hettie's funeral, it's the last thing you will ever do!'

Taggart sat back in frustration, knowing that she meant every word. 'All right. Drive on.'

At the graveside, Taggart's mind was on one thing only – talking to Dawson, an employee of Collins and Son for some thirty years, whose habit of wearing tinted glasses gave him an air of controlled menace. Not wishing to incur Jean's wrath further, Taggart chose to sneak into the kitchen during the after-funeral tea and phone Jardine and Reid, asking them to find out how Dawson came by the keyring. They found Dawson at the funeral parlour with Mary, the receptionist.

'It was in a drawer,' said Dawson, pointing to an old wooden desk. 'That one there. I was just hunting about for a spare keyring and I came across that one.'

'It's been in there at least a year,' added Mary. 'One of these things you keep seeing and stop noticing.'

'A year?' said Jardine.

'Could be two,' replied Mary, giving the matter greater thought.

Jardine was exasperated. 'Look. When we showed you that keyring, nobody recognized it.'

'That one was burnt,' answered Dawson, excusing himself.

Jardine realized they were getting nowhere fast.

Two days later, another silver fox keyring turned up – in the sodden blazer pocket of schoolboy Tony Jacovelli. His body was discovered face down in a golf course water hazard. He had been missing for two days and had been stabbed.

'The keyring was in his lining,' said Jardine, looking at the body. 'Deep down. The killer probably didn't even know it was there.'

'Obligingly careless,' remarked Taggart.

'Question is – what's the connection between him and Telfer?'

'Apart from the fact they both need an undertaker …'

Later that morning, the police visited Jacovelli's school in numbers. The headmaster announced the tragic news at a specially convened assembly, at the end of which glamorous French teacher Françoise Campbell suddenly fainted. Recovering in the headmaster's office, where she was comforted by the head of English, Ian McLaughlin, Mme Campbell was shown the keyring.

'You wouldn't know this, would you?' asked Taggart. 'We found it on Jacovelli. You see, the reason I'm asking is – it comes from France.'

Mme Campbell was adamant that she had never seen it before.

Meanwhile Reid was interviewing one of her pupils, seventeen-year-old Philip Dempster, a keen astronomer who had been seen talking furtively to Jacovelli on the afternoon of his disappearance. At first, Dempster was unable to recollect the subject of their conversation but eventually his memory returned.

'He wanted me to write his French essay for him.'

Reid jotted down the reply but somehow did not quite believe it.

After another chat with Dempster at his home, Taggart decided to call on Mme Campbell. As he entered her flat, he was intent on extracting as much information as possible without seeming to try.

'You know, in my day,' he began, 'French teachers were formidable old dragons. At least mine was.'

'Can I make you some coffee?' she offered.

'No, no thanks. Are you feeling better?'

'Yes, thank you,' she said, soothing her forehead. 'It was just the shock …'

'Of course.' He reached into his pocket. 'Would you take another look at that keyring?'

'I told you. I've never seen it before.'

'Well, it wouldn't hurt you just to look at it once again, would it?'

With some discomfort, she examined the keyring.

'We heard from Jacovelli's parents,' persisted Taggart, 'that he went on a school trip to France last year with you and Mr McLaughlin in charge. We thought he might have picked it up there.'

She handed it back to Taggart. 'I'm sorry, I don't know.'

'You see, it comes from a company near Lille and the school trip never went anywhere near there, did it?'

'No. Not at all. We went to the Dordogne.'

'Nice part of the country, I believe.'

'Yes, I was born there. When I was three, my parents moved to Paris.'

Taggart changed tack. 'Is your husband at home?'

'No. He's away on business. He travels. In fact, I just had a telephone call from him, in France. He's always ringing up, leaving messages.'

'What does he do?'

'He's a consultant – surveillance and security systems. He advises companies what to install.'

Taggart's interest was aroused although he was at pains to play it down. 'Where?'

'All over Europe.'

'Where does he work from?'

'Here. He is self-employed.'

Taggart rose to his feet, ready to leave. As he did so, he stared out of the window and realized that he was looking straight up towards the flat where Philip Dempster lived. Turning, he noticed a photograph of a small boy.

'That yours?'

'Antoine. He was killed in an accident. He ran out between two cars. Two years ago now. Driver didn't stop.'

'I'm sorry.'

Convinced of a French connection, Taggart went to call on Mme Campbell again early the following morning. As he and Reid arrived, the teacher was seen leaving by taxi carrying a large suitcase. Reid followed her while Taggart, confident that the key on the Renard keyring would admit him to Mme Campbell's flat, made his way up the stairs. He was right.

Tony Jacovelli and Philip Dempster.

He searched around inside the flat. On the desk in the bedroom, he noticed a can of air freshener. Trying it, he recognized the fragrance but could not remember from where. Then the telephone rang. He listened to the answerphone message.

The voice said: 'Hello, *mon amour*. Do you know where I am today? Amiens. I wish you could be here with me. After today, I'm going on to Lille – you are not in, so I'll call again tonight. *Au revoir*.'

All the while Taggart was being observed by Jardine through the telescope in the attic observatory of Philip Dempster's high-rise home. Jardine had gone there to establish the boy's feelings about his French teacher and whether he had ever spied on her through the telescope. Initially evasive, and in a hurry to attend Jacovelli's funeral, Philip finally admitted that he had a crush on Mme

Campbell and was trying to protect her. He had been in the habit of peering through the telescope into her bedroom and had even attached a camera to take photographs of her in various states of undress. One night, he had caught her making love with a man whose face he could not see. The lovers had been interrupted by the arrival of another man, presumably her husband. There had been an argument but, at the crucial point, Philip had been called away. When he had returned to the telescope, the blood-stained body of the second man was lying on the floor. All Philip could see was Mme Campbell, also covered in blood, drawing the curtains. End of the peep show.

The only person Philip had confided in was Tony Jacovelli. In return for promising to do Jacovelli's French essay for him, Philip had persuaded Jacovelli to search Mme Campbell's flat for evidence to support the theory that she had murdered her husband. First, Philip had secretly taken a copy of her front-door key. Jacovelli had then slipped the original back into her bag but, having taken a shine to the silver fox keyring, had decided to keep that for himself. Philip had seen Jacovelli break into the flat, but then a man had appeared carrying a large suitcase. Philip had been powerless to help. It was the last time Jacovelli had been seen alive.

Philip had since telephoned Mme Campbell anonymously to assure her that her secret was safe with him. It was undoubtedly that call which had triggered her hasty departure.

McVitie pored over the photographs taken by Philip Dempster. 'Why couldn't he come straight away with these? Instead of playing detective?'

'He's a bit strange, sir,' said Jardine. 'He's a schoolboy with a crush.'

'No clear picture of the other man, sir,' bemoaned Taggart.

Jardine was more optimistic. 'Dempster saw him clearly though. I'm going to bring him back after Jacovelli's funeral to do a photofit.'

McVitie remained restless. 'How does one of these keyrings wind up in Collins, the undertakers?'

'Nice presents, sir,' answered Taggart. 'It's my guess these came to Glasgow via Mrs Campbell's husband, after a business trip to France.'

'Are you sure the body on the floor is that of Mr Campbell?' asked McVitie.

'Yes, sir. I saw photos in the flat.'

'Yet he phoned his wife this morning …'

'*Somebody* phoned her,' corrected Taggart.

To Taggart's irritation, Reid had lost Mme Campbell at Glasgow Central railway station, but not before seeing her deposit the large suitcase in the left luggage office. Jardine prised open the locks with a hammer and screwdriver.

He opened the lid to find a pile of crisp, neatly folded shirts. Delving deeper, he backed off, physically sick. For beneath the shirts lay a polythene-covered human torso, minus head, legs and arms.

'Mr Campbell, I presume?' concluded Taggart.

Dr Andrews sniffed the body. 'It doesn't smell. Probably for one very good reason. It's been embalmed.'

'And where's the rest of him?' enquired McVitie.

'Resting in pieces, sir?' suggested Taggart.

Jardine suddenly realized the implications. 'Jacovelli's funeral – it's being held at Collins and Son. And Dempster's gone there.'

Philip arrived late at the funeral parlour to find Andy Collins on the door. Looking up, he gasped as he recognized Collins as the man in Françoise Campbell's flat. She had deduced that the anonymous call had come from Philip and had warned Collins to that effect. It was Collins who had killed Peter Campbell when the latter had burst in to find him naked in bed with his wife. Smashing a champagne glass to defend himself against the husband's onslaught, Collins had stuck the jagged edge into Campbell's throat. Alec Telfer had seen Collins hiding a plastic bag in a coffin. He did not know that the bag contained Peter Campbell's limbs, but Collins could not take that chance. So Collins arranged for him to have a little accident in his car. Later, discovering a boy hiding beneath the bed and fearing that he would find Campbell's torso in the case, Collins had also felt compelled to murder Tony Jacovelli.

Now it was Philip Dempster's turn to run from Collins. He was chased into the embalming room and then through into the coffin store. He sought refuge in an upright coffin, not daring to breathe for fear of discovery. Armed with a length of rubber tubing, Collins knew he had his prey cornered and opened each lid systematically until he found him.

With the boy trapped in the coffin, Collins tried to strangle him with the tubing but Philip managed to wriggle free with the help of a hefty kick where it hurts most. The struggle continued. Philip grabbed a scalpel. Collins wrested it from him but, in the process, gashed his own hand. Seizing upon his adversary's momentary loss of concentration, Philip succeeded in reaching a container full of embalming fluid and hurled it in Collins's face. Collins immediately sank to the floor, screaming, covering his eyes in agony. Philip rushed out of the embalming room and straight into the arms of Taggart and Jardine.

Collins was duly arrested and, three days later, Mme Campbell, in the finest traditions of a crime passionel, committed suicide by sinking a knife into her breast. Her suicide note read: 'Sometimes life is hard, we do things we

Peter Campbell
meets a sharp end
when he discovers
his wife, Francoise,
in bed with Andy
Collins.

will later regret, but that is not important now. When you find this letter, I will be gone. I will be rejoining my Antoine and my husband, who I still love. Goodbye. Love. I'm sorry.'

If Taggart thought all his troubles were now over, he was sorely mistaken.

'The thing is,' said Jardine with trepidation, 'since Françoise Campbell committed suicide, loverboy Collins has clammed up completely. Refuses to tell us even which coffin he put the head in. Which means we're going to have to exhume the lot.'

'So,' said Taggart, unconcerned. 'Exhume the lot.'

Jardine spelt it out. 'That, unfortunately, includes … your Aunty Hettie, sir.'

Taggart allowed this to sink in for a few moments before silently collecting his coat. He passed McVitie on the way out.

'Going somewhere, Jim?'

'I'm going home to see Jean, sir.' He took a few steps more and turned. 'And then I think I'll emigrate.'

DEATH BENEFITS

Called out to a night-time break-in at Kelvingrove Art Gallery, Jardine's hopes of catching the thieves red-handed were hampered by the late arrival on the scene of Sergeant John Fraser, the gallery's Crime Prevention Officer. He blamed problems with his radio. The crooks' target had been the Bellany Collection of classic modern paintings on loan from the Julius Gallery, New York, but the sound of the alarms had forced them to abandon their haul on the premises. However, despite a huge police presence, they had managed to make good their escape.

The following morning, Taggart, Jardine and Reid were summoned to a murder. The body was that of Julia Fraser, wife of the sergeant. She had been bludgeoned to death with an iron bar in her own bedroom. Various items of skimpy underwear were scattered around the room, although at that stage Dr Andrews was unable to ascertain whether or not she had been sexually assaulted. He put the time of death at around midnight.

Fraser was too distraught to be able to answer many of Taggart's questions. For his part, Taggart probed gently.

'Julia had obviously been out for the evening,' he began. 'She had taken off her make-up and was getting ready for bed. D'you know where she'd been?'

Fraser shook his head.

'There's no evidence of a sexual attack,' continued Taggart. 'Nothing stolen.'

Fraser looked from Taggart to Jardine. 'I can't help thinking, if only …'

'If only what?' asked Taggart.

Jardine intervened. 'The break-in at the gallery, sir. The director wanted Sergeant Fraser's advice. She asked for him to stay on.'

Taggart looked puzzled.

'As Crime Prevention Officer, I advised on the security system for the gallery,' explained Fraser.

'So what time did you find Julia?' pressed Taggart.

Fraser stared blankly at the clock on the wall. 'It must have been about … half-five … six.'

'When you came back to the house, did you find the front door open?'

'No … no, it was locked. I used my key.'

'There was no sign of a break-in. Can you explain that?'

'I haven't really thought about it.'

'Julia wouldn't leave the door unlocked?'

Transmission dates:
16 February
–2 March 1993
Writer: Barry Appleton
Executive producer:
Robert Love
Producer: Paddy Higson
Director: Alan Bell

SUPPORTING CAST:
GEORGE DONALDSON
– Ken Hutchison
MARCO CELLINI
– Ron Donachie
ALEX LANGFORD
– Frederick Warder
JOHN FRASER
– Alexander Morton
CHRISTINE ROCHE
– Siobhan Stanley
CINDY MCKENDRICK
– Caroline Paterson
BOB MCKENDRICK
– Sean Scanlan
JULIA FRASER
– Susie McKenna
TONY MACMILLAN
– Robert Cavanagh
TERRY BAINES
– Iain Andrew
MRS SPICER
– Aileen O'Gorman
SONIA CUMMINGS
– Fiona Chalmers
DUNCAN MILNE
– Brian O'Malley
REV. PETER ARMSTRONG
– Cameron Stewart
MRS ARMSTRONG
– Bridget McCann

'No,' replied Fraser, tiring of Taggart's questions. 'She's very particular about things like that.'

'So. Julia either let the killer in or he had a key?'

'No. That's not possible. I … I can't believe that!' A thought flashed through his mind – despite his grief, he was still a policeman at heart. 'Wait a minute! She misplaced her keys a few weeks ago.'

'Did she find them?' asked Jardine.

'She didn't mention it again. I took it she'd found them. If she hadn't, I'd have changed the locks.'

Fraser did volunteer one other piece of information – that Julia's best friend was a woman called Cindy McKendrick, who lived up the road. He said they went Scottish country dancing together. Cindy was well known to Taggart. A plain woman in her early thirties, her face a make-up free zone, she was the estranged wife of an ex-colleague, Inspector Bob McKendrick. He was now a member of the Regional Crime Squad in Manchester, and, coincidentally, currently in charge of the investigation into the break-in at the gallery, as well as a number of other major art thefts throughout the UK. McKendrick had left Glasgow under a cloud four years earlier, transferred after a young policewoman had alleged that he had sexually assaulted her at a promotion party.

Taggart renewed his acquaintance with Cindy McKendrick, who said that Julia Fraser had been over at her house the previous evening until about 10.30pm. The interview was cut short when Taggart spotted the rugged figure of Bob McKendrick stepping from a car outside the station. Cindy was horrified at the prospect of meeting him again and had to be whisked out by another exit. Taggart too had little time for McKendrick, even though he was godfather to the McKendricks' children.

The post-mortem on Julia Fraser revealed no evidence of a sexual attack. Slight bruising on her right hand suggested she had offered token resistance. Taggart was sure she knew her killer. He needed to know more about her lifestyle, particularly any boyfriends.

'You don't get dressed up in fancy knickers to go Highland dancing, do you, Michael?'

Jardine smiled. 'It's an interesting thought, sir.'

'I want a thorough search of the house,' ordered Taggart. 'Anything that will give us a clue to Julia's background.'

Meanwhile Reid was deployed to win Fraser's confidence. They went for a walk in the park together and Fraser began to open up. But there was no hint of an unhappy marriage – quite the opposite.

'The last eighteen months were wonderful,' Fraser told her. 'Things had never been better between us.'

The breakthrough Taggart needed came with the discovery of a pocket diary, tucked away at the back of a dressing-table. It belonged to Julia Fraser and contained a list of hastily scribbled names and telephone numbers as well as a business card from a rather sleazy Glasgow club called Le Kilt.

Taggart and Jardine entered the club as an Egyptian queen in full Anubis mask was rehearsing her strip routine. Among the customers was Marco Cellini, a local hood who passed himself off as a businessman. Backstage, Taggart sought out the manager, Tony Macmillan.

'Do you know a woman by the name of Julia Fraser?'

Macmillan shook his head. 'Sorry.'

'She may have been a customer,' continued Taggart. 'She had your card amongst her possessions.'

'Sorry. We don't cater for women. Have you tried the tea shop in the High Street?'

Taggart did not appreciate the joke. 'Don't be clever, son.'

Jardine showed Macmillan a photograph of Julia. He glanced at it and smiled.

'You recognize her?' asked Taggart hopefully.

'Gina … Gina de Silva. Gina's one of my girls. A stripper.'

'A stripper?' repeated an incredulous Taggart.

'Aye, she does a good wee number. A bit nervous perhaps, but good.'

'Well, for your information,' said Taggart firmly, 'Gina is doing a good wee number in the city mortuary at this moment.'

Marco Cellini,
underworld
'businessman'.

A shaken Macmillan said he did not know 'Gina' that well but suggested Taggart talk to the Egyptian queen, a girl called Danielle. Taggart and Jardine waited patiently outside the dressing-room until 'Danielle' emerged. They knew her better as Cindy McKendrick!

Cindy revealed that she and Julia had been stripping at the club for four or five months. It was just a bit of fun and excitement. On the night she was murdered, Julia had left Le Kilt with Terry Baines, the young gopher at the club. Terry, who was one sandwich short of a picnic, had been hopelessly infatuated with Julia.

As Terry was brought in for questioning, Taggart met Bob McKendrick in the station yard. McKendrick was having a white car examined for fingerprints.

'Your lads slipped up,' said McKendrick with satisfaction. 'This Escort was stolen from the car park behind the gallery the night of the break-in. Used as a getaway.'

'The car park was covered,' said Taggart. 'By Sergeant Fraser.'

'Fraser? Now there's a coincidence,' said McKendrick, his voice heavy with sarcasm.

The frightened Terry pleaded with Taggart to believe that he had nothing to do with Julia's murder. He insisted that he had just dropped her off that night – he had not even gone into the house.

'All I did was put my hand on her thigh,' he sobbed. 'She let me do that sometimes. She liked teasing me. I didn't mind. But I didn't kill her!'

'Tell us about the others,' said Jardine. 'Others like yourself, who she maybe teased a little. Someone who may have come on a bit strong.'

Terry buried his face in his hands. There was a lingering silence. He took a deep breath. 'He and Julia talked a lot. Sometimes they left the club together. When I was busy, I couldn't take her home.'

'Who're we talking about, Terry?'

'I don't know his name. Julia said he does kitchens. Has a shop, somewhere in the city centre. Drives a Jaguar.'

Fraser, stunned by his wife's double life, did not recognize any of the twenty names on Julia's list. Reid's attempts to trace them proved equally unsuccessful. One, Isobel Spicer, had died just two days earlier after falling in front of a train. She had been planning to go on a world cruise with her mother. Then news came through that another, mechanic Greg Cummings, had just been blown to pieces by an explosion in his lock-up garage. The car he was working on had fallen off the jack, trapping him and rupturing the fuel tank. His welding torch had obviously dropped too close to the leaking tank and the whole place went up. It bore all the hallmarks of an accidental death but, following hot on the heels of the Spicer case, it not surprisingly aroused Taggart's suspicions.

The mystery kitchen designer turned out to be George Donaldson, a quiet, smartly dressed man with cash-flow problems and a broken marriage. As Terry Baines was released, Donaldson was brought in for questioning.

He maintained that he did not know Julia Fraser that well. 'I took her out a few times for dinner. That was some time ago. I didn't know she was married until I saw the newspaper.'

'Did you ever have sex with Julia?' said Jardine.

'I know this may sound silly, but she wasn't that kind of girl.'

'What kind of girl was she?'

'Good company. Intelligent, bubbly. I liked her a lot.'

'What time did you leave Le Kilt on the night of the murder?' asked Taggart.

'About midnight.'

'Can anyone verify that?'

'Mr Cellini.'

'Marco Cellini?' checked Taggart, knowing full well that an alibi from a crook like Cellini was virtually worthless.

'I designed a kitchen for him,' said Donaldson. 'He had some minor electrical problem. I went and fixed it.'

That evening, a sheepish-looking Donaldson returned to the station.

Jardine ushered him into Taggart's office. 'Mr Donaldson has something to tell us.'

Donaldson sat at the desk. 'I didn't tell the complete truth about Julia. I knew you would find out sooner or later.'

Taggart eyed him quizzically. 'And what would we find out sooner or later, Mr Donaldson?'

Donaldson steeled himself for the announcement. 'That I was having an affair with Julia.'

Taggart looked at Jardine. His irritated expression said it all. Taggart threw off his jacket, clumsily loosened his tie and prepared to take a statement. Another late night.

Donaldson talked for nearly two hours about his relationship with Julia. 'Hesitant … that's the only way I can describe it … It never really got any further than holding hands and a few kisses. I know this may be difficult for you to understand …'

Taggart cut in. 'You never made love to her?'

'No!'

'And you've never been to her house?'

'Never.'

'And there is nothing else you want to tell us?'

By now, Donaldson too was exhausted. 'I've told you everything.'

Taggart exploded. 'You haven't told us any more than we already know!'

'I had to get it off my chest!' protested Donaldson.

'If you need peace of mind, go see a priest!' growled Taggart. 'I'm not in the business of cleansing souls! What I want are hard facts that will help solve this case before anybody else is killed!' He jabbed an accusing finger at Donaldson. 'You've wasted my time.' The finger became a dismissive gesture of the arm. 'Get him out of here!'

Jardine and Reid continued to explore all avenues. Greg Cummings's widow, Sonia, revealed that, like Donaldson, her late husband was separated and had money problems. He had borrowed heavily from a loan shark –

Cellini – and had been given a strange warning by an anonymous woman shortly before his death. According to Sonia, the woman had said that someone was after Greg and that he should go into hiding.

Cellini was a stocky man, fattened by the fruits of the Glasgow underworld. He admitted having leant on Cummings a little. 'It's no secret I had to duff him up a wee bit. Nothing personal you understand, just a warning. There was no need for any hard stuff. The man appreciated the position he'd got himself in and came up with the money at the eleventh hour.'

'He paid up?' said Taggart.

'In cash. The full amount.'

Jardine showed Cellini the photograph of Julia Fraser.

'Do you know this girl?'

'Sure. A stripper at Le Kilt.

'She was murdered a few nights ago,' interjected Taggart.

Reid and Jardine attempt to find the missing link from Julia Fraser's list.

'And you think I'm responsible for every crime in this city?'

Taggart gave a knowing look. 'A damn good percentage.'

Cellini was innocence personified. 'Every night this week I have been with my solicitor working out a deal on the takeover of a casino. There's no profit in violence, Mr Taggart. If I can avoid it, I do. The past is past. I'm trying hard to live down a reputation I didn't deserve.'

Taggart snorted his disdain.

Reid continued to make her way through Julia Fraser's list. Some names on it were uncontactable but at least one other had met an untimely end. A girl called Jess Nathan had drowned three months before, while painting the boat on which she lived with her boyfriend, Duncan Milne. The dilapidated boat had been all the young couple could afford.

There was still no obvious link between the names on the list, however, and the team were becoming dispirited. 'Julia knew the connection,' Taggart reminded them. 'That's why she was killed.'

Later that day, they were nearly able to cross another name off the list – that of motorcycle courier Danny Robertson. Going out on a job wearing his shiny new set of leathers, he was critically injured in a collision with a van.

Taggart and Jardine considered the situation over a leisurely drink.

'Somewhere,' said Taggart. 'Julia had seen a list of names and telephone numbers which she hurriedly copied. Now where would she have access to those names?' He took a long, deep sigh. 'I'm convinced Cindy holds the key to this.'

Before he could expand on his theory, Taggart was rudely interrupted by a television news report about an armed robbery earlier that afternoon at the Kelvingrove Gallery. Masked raiders had ambushed the van preparing to ship the Bellany Collection back to New York. The robbery had been expertly planned and executed.

Following up his hunch, Taggart visited Cindy McKendrick at her house. He found her battered and bruised, the result of a visit from her husband. She blamed Taggart for telling Bob about her alternative lifestyle at Le Kilt. Taggart swore he had done no such thing.

Hoping he was in the clear, Taggart quietly popped the question.

'Cindy, I need your help. If you're holding anything back about Julia ...'

His timing was by no means perfect. 'Julia! Julia! To hell with bloody Julia!' she screamed.

'I've got to know.'

'Can't you just leave it!'

'No.'

Cindy gazed into space. To Taggart, it seemed like an eternity. Finally, she broke her silence.

'She entertained ... at private parties.'

'What parties?'

'Cellini. He loved the idea of screwing a copper's wife. It gave him a thrill. He had some kind of hold on Julia.'

'Like what?'

'Drugs, I don't know. Whenever she came back from one of those parties, she said she felt dirty ... disgusted with herself.'

'How did she come to meet Cellini?'

'The club. It's his club.'

'Cellini owns Le Kilt?'

'One of his recent acquisitions. Tony is only a front man. Didn't you know that?'

Danny Robertson's life still hung in the balance.

'Sir,' Taggart told McVitie, 'I want a bodyguard on every person left on Julia's list.'

'We've yet to prove these deaths are anything other than accidents,' protested McVitie. 'You see my position, Jim?'

Taggart was adamant. 'I don't care if it takes a bloody battalion of the Queen's Own Highlanders. I want these people under a twenty-four-hour guard!'

But the move came too late to prevent the demise of another on the list. Peter Armstrong, a young Church of Scotland minister, plunged to his death from the belltower of his church. Mrs Armstrong was remarkably composed – even for a minister's wife. She mentioned that Peter had received a telephone call shortly before his death – from a newspaper photographer wanting some shots to accompany an article on the belltower appeal.

'Did you see this photographer?' asked Reid, sipping the cup of tea she had made to lubricate the interview.

'I doubt whether he turned up,' confessed Mrs Armstrong. 'If the truth be told, there was very little interest in the appeal.' She leaned forward in a conspiratorial manner. 'I'll let you into a little secret, Miss Reid. The two-and-a-half thousand pounds already collected was not the result of anonymous donations, but money from an insurance policy Peter surrendered. His commitment was absolute, you see.'

Taggart decided to raid one of Cellini's private parties. Literally caught with his trousers down, Cellini offered a different appraisal of Julia and Cindy, saying that it was Cindy and not Julia who was always eager to earn a bit more on the side. He insisted that Julia was never at any of his parties. Much as it went against the grain, Taggart was inclined to believe him.

Taggart was sick of being lied to. At Julia's funeral, he made a point of cornering Cindy as she left the graveside. Reluctantly, she confirmed Cellini's version of events.

'Nobody can do her any further harm,' said Cindy, ashamed to look Taggart directly in the eye. 'She's safe away from it all.'

Taggart bursts in on Cellini's undercover activities.

She quickened her step, hoping to leave Taggart behind.

He responded. 'And that gives you the right?'

Cindy stopped. 'Jim, I'm the one that's left to suffer the humiliation of all this, not Julia.'

'And that makes it okay? Transferring your guilt and shame to a dead person.'

'I have to think about the children.' She turned and set off again. 'Now will you please leave me alone?'

Right from the outset, Bob McKendrick had suspected that John Fraser was involved in Julia's murder, and now, armed with the tapes from the gallery security cameras showing the first robbery attempt and also Fraser's old army record, Taggart too began to lean that way. It became clear that it was Fraser who had stolen the Ford Escort – from the gallery car park – whilst his army file revealed that when he was stationed in Germany, he had nearly killed a man who had tried to chat up Julia in a bar. The psychiatrist at the time remarked that Fraser had abnormal or violent social behaviour when aggravated.

In the meantime, McKendrick has hauled in a suspect for the robbery – professional art thief Alex Langford.

McKendrick was looking forward to the contest, a battle of wits between battle-hardened policeman and master criminal.

'This job has your name written all over it,' McKendrick told Langford with Taggart in silent attendance. 'I can place you in at least eight other cities at the time of similar art thefts.'

Langford knew McKendrick had to do better than that. 'A coincidence, I can assure you.'

'This time you had inside information. Somebody who either knew the transport arrangements or was in a position to find out.'

McKendrick blindly held out his hand to a woman detective. She handed him an envelope and he spread the contents, a series of blown-up photographs, across the desk in front of Langford. They showed Langford and Fraser strolling in the Botanical Gardens.

Art thief Alex Langford attempts to blackmail Sergeant John Fraser into revealing the security system for his next job.

Langford was too seasoned a criminal to go down without a fight. Showing no sign of panic, he named his girlfriend, Christine Roche, as his alibi. He had regularly loved and left Christine, using her conveniently between robberies. She knew nothing of his criminal activities – he had always told her he restored old paintings for a living. He had never said for whom ...

Jardine rounds up the guests after Cellini's private party.

'She will vouch that I was in her company at the time of the break-in and the robbery,' stated Langford confidently.

'You sure about that?'

'Positive.'

At that, McKendrick played his trump card and wheeled in Christine Roche. The significance of her presence was all too obvious. Langford was mortified.

'I'm sorry, Alex,' she said. 'You left me once too many times.'

McKendrick triumphantly turned to Taggart. 'He's all yours.'

Langford soon opened up about Fraser. Reading about Julia Fraser's murder, Langford had recognized a photograph of her husband as the policeman he had seen steal an Escort on the night of the abortive robbery. At the time, Langford had been making good his escape. Putting two and two together, he had deduced that Fraser had driven home and killed his own wife. Langford had decided to blackmail Fraser. In return for Langford's silence about the Escort, Fraser had furnished him with the security information which had finally enabled him to snatch the Bellany Collection.

No sooner had Taggart ordered that Fraser be brought in for further questioning than at last a link began to emerge between the names on Julia's list. It was sparked by a phone call from Sonia Cummings, who had taken quite a shine to Jardine. She had been curious to know how Greg had managed to pay off the £3,000 loan to Cellini. Now she had found out – he had cashed in an endowment policy. Alarm bells began to ring.

'That's strange,' said Reid. 'Mrs Armstrong mentioned that her husband had cashed in an endowment policy to help the belltower appeal. And Isobel Spicer raised money for her intended world cruise.'

Jardine took up the train of thought. 'Milne, Jess's boyfriend. He said they needed cash to repair the houseboat ...'

Jardine went straight round to talk to Mrs Spicer. She revealed that Isobel had auctioned an endowment policy to pay for the planned cruise. Jardine and Reid were certain that they were on to something.

'We've established so far that twelve people on Julia's list had recently cashed in their insurance policies,' Jardine told Taggart excitedly.

As he spoke, it became thirteen. Reid learned that Danny Robertson, still lying in a coma, had auctioned a policy to buy a new motorcycle and leathers.

'Exactly the same,' reported Reid as she came off the phone. 'Danny was offered a lousy surrender value by his insurance company, so he auctioned his endowment policy to get a much better deal. He read about it in the newspaper.'

McVitie knew all about the practice. 'Mendleson Brothers, the auctioneers off Queen Street. That's their speciality.'

Taggart and Jardine hurried round to Mendlesons to find an auction in progress. Afterwards, they asked the auctioneer about the sort of people who bought up insurance policies.

'Mainly brokers,' replied the auctioneer. 'Secondhand policies are a very good investment. The new owner continues the payments as if he or she were the policy holder. Full value of the policy is then paid out by the respective insurance company on the maturity date, with, of course, the bonuses that accumulate each year.'

'That could be a lot of money?' said Taggart, wide-eyed.

'Oh yes, thousands. A true investment for anybody with the foresight.'

Taggart asked the auctioneer to check his records to find the names on Julia's list. Leafing through the leather-bound ledger, the auctioneer stopped at a page.

'Here we are ... Four policies purchased on the same day. Spicer, Robertson, Cummings ... and Armstrong.'

'Who was the bidder?'

'They were purchased by an agent ... Miss Gina de Rosa.'

Taggart and Jardine traded smug glances. Taggart showed the auctioneer a photograph of Julia.

'Yes. That's her.'

'Who did she represent?'

The auctioneer referred to his books once more. 'A company called Castel Investments.'

Taggart noted the address and made for the door. As he reached the exit, he paused and turned.

'What happens if the original policy holder dies before the term of insurance expires?'

'A windfall for the new owner,' answered the auctioneer.

'You mean the death benefit is payable in full?' reiterated Jardine.

'As I said before, gentlemen. An excellent investment for somebody with foresight.'

With Fraser still on the loose, Taggart and Jardine drove away from the auction house, putting together the pieces of the jigsaw. Suddenly, Jardine swung the car into a U-turn.

'What are you doing, Michael?' shouted Taggart.

Jardine pointed to the drive of a secluded Victorian building which was in a state of disrepair. 'Donaldson's Jaguar. There it is. And Fraser's probably with him. He read Donaldson's statement – yes – in your office. He's going to hunt him down, isn't he? You know what happened to the other chap that just chatted to his wife …'

'Very good, Michael! Now can you just check if by chance this is the office of Castel Investments?'

It was. Donaldson had opened the business as a little sideline. But now, just as Jardine thought, he was being threatened by the insanely jealous Fraser. Donaldson pleaded that his relationship with Julia had been purely business, and related how she bought insurance policies at the auction house for him.

Donaldson switched on the computer. Fraser nodded towards the screen.

'How does this help me find the man she was having an affair with?'

Donaldson was desperately trying to buy time. 'One of the original policy holders may have attended the auction to see who bid for his or her particular policy … Saw Julia and struck up a relationship.' He casually stepped back and gestured towards the data on the screen. 'There. These are the names of the policy holders.'

Fraser peered at the screen and quickly realized that the names – Spicer, Cummings, etc. – were all people who had died suspiciously. As Fraser turned to confront Donaldson, the latter seized a pair of scissors and stabbed him in the shoulder. Donaldson ran down the stairs, only to find his escape route blocked by Jardine. He headed back upstairs and attempted to wrench open the window leading to the fire escape. It was jammed. As Jardine appeared at the door, Donaldson made a dash for the other window, but the weak floor gave way and he fell through, crashing at the feet of Taggart and Fraser in the office below.

As Donaldson was removed on a stretcher, the forlorn figure of John Fraser leaned against the side of a police car, his shirt bloodstained and a heavy dressing across his chest. Taggart came over to talk to him.

'Julia found out what he was up to,' said Fraser. 'That's why he killed her.'

'You should have come to me from the start,' chided Taggart.

'If I'd told you I went back that night to catch them together, I would have been your number one suspect. I needed time to track Donaldson down.'

'If it's any consolation, she was never unfaithful to you.'

'I've known, deep down I've always known. It was my jealousy that blinded me to the fact.'

Taggart nodded knowingly. 'It's something you'll have to learn to live with.'

REVIEWING THE EVIDENCE
– A COMPLETE EPISODE GUIDE

Killer

Eileen Ballantyne, a young woman of twenty, is found strangled one winter's morning on the banks of Glasgow's River Kelvin. A chunk of hair has been cut from her head. Detective Chief Inspector Jim Taggart from the Northern Division, Glasgow CID, is assigned to the case, assisted by Detective Sergeant Peter Livingstone, a graduate newly transferred from Edinburgh. Taggart is uneasy about the case since the victim is

**Transmission dates:
6–20 September 1983
Writer: Glenn Chandler
Producer: Robert Love
Director: Laurence Moody**

more or less the same type and age as his own daughter, Alison. Suspects include Billy Dalgleish, the dead girl's boyfriend, Martin Inglis, the jogger who stumbled across the body, and Alec McGowan, a man with a history of offences against girls. Then there is Michael Boyd, who lives with his school-cleaner wife, Liz, in a high-rise block of flats overlooking the murder site. Boyd seems to be showing an unhealthy interest in the crime. Two days later, a second girl, video shop manageress Susan Maguire, is found strangled on a canal bank. She too has had a clump of hair cut away. Taggart closes in on the shop owner, Charlie Paterson, with whom Susan was having an affair, but, to his intense displeasure, is warned off by his boss, Superintendent Murray, a golfing chum of Paterson. Michael Boyd's sinister presence at Eileen Ballantyne's funeral plus the discovery on wasteland near the Clyde of the body of a third girl, prostitute Crystal Kent, also with hair shorn, briefly lead Taggart in a different direction. But when hiring out a video from Paterson's shop, Boyd recognizes him as the man he saw on the Kelvin Walkway on the night Eileen Ballantyne was murdered. When Susan Maguire's bag turns up, a note makes Taggart too realize that Paterson is definitely the killer. Paterson had eliminated Susan because she had been blackmailing him over the earlier murder of his wife's lover. He strangled the other two women to make Susan's death appear to be the work of a serial killer. Now Paterson is being blackailed for a second time – by Michael Boyd. Taggart races to the scene of the 'drop', but not in time to prevent Paterson strangling Boyd, the joker in the pack.

SUPPORTING CAST:
DS PETER LIVINGSTONE
– Neil Duncan
SUPT. ROBERT MURRAY
– Tom Watson
BILLY DALGLEISH
– Vincent Friell
JEAN TAGGART
– Harriet Buchan
ALISON TAGGART
– Geraldine Alexander
DR STEPHEN ANDREWS
– Robert Robertson
MICHAEL BOYD
– Gerard Kelly
LIZ BOYD
– Linda Muchan
ALEC MCGOWAN
– Frank Wylie
MARTIN INGLIS
– Bertie Scott
CHARLIE PATERSON
– Roy Hanlon
PATRICIA PATERSON
– Anne Kidd

Dead Ringer

Transmission dates:
2–16 July 1985
Writer: Glenn Chandler
Producer: Robert Love
Director: Laurence Moody

SUPPORTING CAST:
JOSEPHINE PEEBLES
– Colette O'Neil
RONNIE MACISAAC
– Jake D'Arcy
DAVID BALFOUR
– Alexander Morton
MIKE BALFOUR
– John McGlynn
JUNE BALFOUR
– Maureen Beattie

(Previous page):
Les Farquar and
Bunny Cotter turn
up at the funeral of
Eileen Ballantyne but
prove to be red
herrings.

When the skeletal remains of a dismembered body are found beneath the floorboards of a house being renovated in Maryhill, a wedding ring and a handbag bearing a thumbprint result in the remains being identified as those of Margaret Balfour – a woman who went missing after being abducted from her car in a layby on the road to Largs in 1975. Her husband, David Balfour, has since been serving a life sentence for her murder, largely due to circumstantial evidence suggesting he had buried his wife near the coast. Taggart and Livingstone discover that at the time of the abduction, the house was a hostel for ex-convicts run by a wealthy benefactor named Josephine Peebles, who is now married to ex-armed robber Ronnie MacIsaac. The room beneath where the remains were found was used by one Frederick O'Donnell, who borrowed Ms Peebles' car on the night of Margaret Balfour's disappearance. O'Donnell is now dead. With doubts about the conviction now emerging, David Balfour is released from prison and Taggart – the detective on the original case and the man who obtained Balfour's 'confession' – is pilloried in the press for his incompetence. The investigation takes another turn when nine-month-old Christopher Balfour, son of David's brother Mike, is kidnapped. A ransom of £50,000 is demanded. Taggart tries to trap the kidnapper, but the operation goes wrong, putting the child's life in grave danger. The only part of Margaret Balfour's remains still missing is the skull. Acting on a hunch, Taggart has the river dredged. The corresponding skull turns up, but the dentures show that it is definitely not that of Margaret Balfour. Taggart realizes that he has been the victim of an intricate web of double-deceit, a murderous insurance plot involving David and Michael Balfour and Michael's wife, June.

Murder in Season

Transmission dates:
23 July–6 August 1985
Writer: Glenn Chandler
Producer: Haldane Duncan
Director:
Peter Barber-Fleming

SUPPORTING CAST:
SUPT. JACK MCVITIE
– Iain Anders
ELEANOR SAMSON
– Isla Blair
FRANK MULHOLLAND
– Andrew Keir
JOHN SAMSON
– Martin Cochrane
JIMMY PETRIE
– Douglas Sannachan
DOROTHY MILNER
– Eileen Nicholas
ALISON TAGGART
– Leigh Biagi
GRAEME SAMSON
– Danny Hignett

Internationally renowned opera singer Eleanor Samson has returned home to Glasgow to sing with the Scottish Opera and to attempt a reconciliation with her estranged husband, John. However, the latter has been having an affair with his secretary, Kirsty King. Following a bitter confrontation with Eleanor Samson, Miss King is found murdered in the burnt-out remnants of John Samson's new boat. Eleanor becomes the prime suspect, especially since traces of petrol are found on her clothing. Eleanor's father, Frank Mulholland, witnessed the fire, and his silence suggests to Taggart and Livingstone that he is shielding his daughter. It transpires that Kirsty King has also had affairs with her previous employer, Ted Maxwell, and John Samson's son Graeme. When John discovers Graeme's secret, he throws him out of the house. Eleanor arrives later to find John Samson shot through the head with his own shotgun. It points to suicide, but Taggart suspects murder. Meanwhile, Keith Brennan plans to have his wife, Lilly, murdered so that he can sell the run-down pub which was left to her by her father and which developers are keen to acquire. He hires an unemployed youth, Jimmy Petrie, to carry out the killing for £5,000. Keith's alibi is that he was collecting his wife's clothes from the dry cleaner's, an establishment also patronized by Frank Mulholland. But on the appointed afternoon, Lilly has gone to see Dr MacNaughten about her varicose veins, and when Petrie arrives at the pub he comes face to face with her assistant, Olive McQueen. Petrie murders her and flees, dumping Keith Brennan's watch in a nearby canal. The police find the watch with Petrie's fingerprints on it and arrest Jimmy. While Brennan ponders why he too has not been picked up, Frank Mulholland suffers a heart attack and dies. The key to the case turns out to be the dry cleaner, Dorothy Milner. In league with Dr MacNaughten, she has been extracting money from people's wills by fraudulent means.

KEITH BRENNAN
– Ronnie Letham
LILLY BRENNAN
– Katherine Stark
DR MACNAUGHTEN
– Ken Stott
OLIVE MCQUEEN
– Dorothy Paul
TED MAXWELL
– Derek Anders
KIRSTY KING
– Brenda Haldane

Knife Edge

(See Chapter 6 'THE MARYHILL FILES' page 40)

Death Call

Livingstone keeps in trim for the case with a spot of judo.

Wealthy land owner Robert Russell and his glamorous German-born wife, Eva, live at Dalnabreck golf club, which they are planning to convert into an American-style country club – a move that does not endear them to the members. In the meantime, the Russells are about to leave Glasgow for a lengthy stay in Switzerland. Robert collects £40,000 from his bank while Eva does some last-minute shopping. In her haste, she leaves a purchase at Elder's the chemist, where young shop assistant Jamie McCormack takes it upon himself to return it personally. At the golf club, Jamie spots the money in a leather holdall, shortly before the Russells receive an important phone call. The next morning, Eva is found strangled, under the water at the edge of a reservoir, her body weighted down with the luggage cases. The money is missing. Looking into the possibility that Robert Russell has done a 'Lord Lucan', Taggart, Livingstone

Transmission dates: 2–16 September 1986
Writer: Glenn Chandler
Producer: Robert Love
Director: Haldane Duncan

SUPPORTING CAST:
DET. SGT. FORFAR
– Stuart Hepburn
ROBERT RUSSELL
– John Cairney
EVA RUSSELL
– Brigitte Kahn
HELEN MENDOZA
– Jill Meager
SANDY RUSSELL
– Michael Carter
MARIE BURNS
– Juliet Cadzow

and Detective Sergeant Forfar interview Sandy Russell, Robert's unsuccessful artist brother, and Sandy's fiery sculptress girlfriend, Marie Burns. The latter reveals that Eva talked about a son by her previous marriage and that the son is living somewhere in Germany. The police also learn, from the Russells' solicitor, Helen Mendoza (an old university flame of Livingstone), about Jamie's visit. Jamie in turn boasts about his involvement in a murder enquiry to his Irish girlfriend, Kathleen Kelly, who works at a small guest house run by Frances Greig. Soon Robert Russell turns up, in a barn near the reservoir. He is barely alive. Forfar alone hears his dying words, which are 'the boy …'. Post-mortems show that Robert and Eva Russell were drugged with a fast-acting barbiturate powder before being strangled. Jamie becomes the chief suspect and Forfar, convinced of his guilt, manufactures evidence to frame him. Forfar's attempt fails and Taggart throws him bodily out of the office. Meanwhile, two more bodies are discovered – in the boot of a car dredged from the Clyde. They are those of Keith and Janice

JAMIE MCCORMACK
– Alan Cumming
FRANCES GREIG
– Anne Kristen
ANDREW MCCORMACK
– Charles Kearney
AGNES COOK
– Irene Sunters
KATHLEEN KELLY
– Julie Graham

Brown, who had absconded from Edinburgh with a large amount of cash. They had been drugged with the same barbiturate as the Russells and strangled. Taggart sets out to find a link between the two couples and in doing so exposes the guest-house owner, Frances Greig. She had been selling surrogate babies and then killing the couples when they arrived with the money.

The Killing Philosophy
(See Chapter 6 'THE MARYHILL FILES' page 54)

Unfortunate couple, Maggie and Colin Davidson.

Transmission dates:
9–23 September 1987
Writer: Glenn Chandler
Producer: Robert Love
Director: Alan Macmillan

SUPPORTING CAST:
MAGGIE DAVIDSON
– Annette Crosbie
COLIN DAVIDSON
– Paul Young
FATHER MARTIN
– Colin Gourley
TOMMY CAMPBELL
– Vincent Friell
MALCOLM MCWHINNIE
– Jimmy Chisholm
PAT CONNOLLY
– Ron Donachie
SHONA FREEDMAN
– Katy Hale
DOUGLAS ABERNATHY
– Mel Donald

Funeral Rites

Dentist Colin Davidson makes two attempts to murder his wife, Maggie. Both attempts fail, but when Maggie injures herself by falling downstairs she is taken to hospital, where she meets up with her friend, Jean Taggart. In the course of conversation, Maggie recommends a visiting hairdresser, Malcolm McWhinnie. After Douglas Abernathy, a seedy private detective, has been attacked and burned to death by someone wearing surgical gloves, Taggart and Jardine are called to the scene. It emerges that Abernathy was a satanist. Kenny Forfar, now a civilian and assisting Abernathy in his detective agency, is trying to trace fifteen-year-old Shona Freedman, who has gone missing from a commune. Forfar is also being hounded by gravedigger Pat Connolly, who is anxious to find Abernathy. On the way home from the Cawder Arms public house, Connolly's throat is slit with a razor and he is buried alive in an open grave. Fellow gravedigger Tommy Campbell, a young deaf and dumb lad, discovers the body and indicates to Taggart that he once saw Abernathy and Connolly talking together about money they had received to commit murder. Strangely, the fingerprints on the razor are those of the dead Abernathy. On Easter Saturday Davidson, too, becomes a victim: having been told by Maggie that a patient has phoned needing emergency treatment, Davidson goes to the surgery, where he is brutally murdered by somebody wearing surgical gloves. Near the body, Taggart examines photographs of Abernathy and Shona (whom he found and coerced into posing for pornographic pictures), and a club from Abernathy's flat. Both the club and the surgery telephone are covered with Douglas Abernathy's fingerprints. Taggart realizes that the fingerprints must have been planted on the murder weapons to make it look like Abernathy was still alive. Eventually, it dawns on Taggart that the solution to the murders lies much closer to home – with Jean's friend, Maggie. She is a secret heroin addict and, in order to fund her habit, she needed her husband's money. So she had hired Abernathy and Connolly to kill him. When they had tried to blackmail her instead, she had employed the seemingly friendly local hairdresser Malcolm McWhinnie to murder them. Those jobs complete, McWhinnie had then proceeded to murder Colin Davidson, the original target.

Cold Blood

Ruth Wilson, a glamorous woman in her late thirties and director of a cosmetics manufacturing firm, arrives by train at the Scottish Exhibition and Conference Centre, which is hosting a large beauty convention. Brushing aside animal rights protesters, she goes to the car park where her husband, George Wilson, is sitting in his car and shoots him dead through the windscreen. Taggart and Jardine are called to the scene to conduct what appears to be an open-and-shut case. Mrs Wilson does not regret the shooting, claiming that her husband was having an affair with Geraldine Keenan, manageress of his beauty centre. But Dr Andrews diagnoses that George Wilson was already dead when Ruth shot him. He had been stabbed in the back. There are signs of theft – a missing wallet and wristwatch – and all the evidence points to the killer being a hitch-hiker whom the deceased had picked up on his journey to Glasgow. This theory is supported by the statements of Stuart Hardie and Duncan Stoddart, who run a nearby mobile café and recall selling George Wilson two cheeseburgers shortly after six o'clock that morning. Ruth Wilson tells Taggart that Ricki Keenan, Geraldine's brother and a snooker professional, was lent £60,000 by her husband, a debt which has never been repaid. Wilson's missing watch had been a present from Ricki Keenan. When Donny McGregor, a twenty-one-year-old youth with a red triangle tattoo on his left hand, is seen burning George Wilson's wallet and trying to sell the wristwatch, the investigation takes a new twist. A youth with a red triangle tattoo is wanted in connection with the robbery of a motorist on the A74, but Ricki Keenan gets to McGregor before the police can. Concealing a large kitchen knife, Keenan shares a fairground ride with McGregor. They struggle on the big wheel and McGregor falls to his death. Keenan maintains that it was an accident. Jardine pursues a Chinese connection and learns that George Wilson was sent a birthday card by a Miss Lin Chang. But the vital clue is provided by Hardie and Stoddart at the mobile café. Taggart realizes that Ruth Wilson *had* been around earlier on the day of the murder and that it was she who had stabbed her husband. And it was she who was having the affair – with Ricki Keenan. But before Taggart can apprehend her, she kills again, callously pushing Keenan to his death off a dam wall.

Gun-toting Ruth Wilson.

Transmission date:
31 December 1987
Writer: Glenn Chandler
Producer: Robert Love
Director: Haldane Duncan

SUPPORTING CAST:
RUTH WILSON
– Diane Keen
DONNY MCGREGOR
– Leonard O'Malley
RICKI KEENAN
– Freddie Boardley
GERALDINE KEENAN
– Margo Gunn
STUART HARDIE
– Paul Morrow
DUNCAN STODDART
– Kenneth Lindsay
LIN CHANG
– Choy Ling-Man
MRS MCVITIE
– Mona Bruce

Dead Giveaway

Minicab firm owner Robert Higgison returns to his Glasgow home from a job which took him to Fort William to find that his son Joe, a member of Jardine's church youth club, has died under mysterious circumstances. It is not the first recent death in the family – Robert's wife also apparently perished from food poisoning. Enquiries lead to Tibor Meray, a Hungarian food manufacturer, who

Transmission dates:
7–21 September 1988
Writer: Glenn Chandler
Producer: Peter
Barber-Fleming
Director: Alan Macmillan

Taggart interviews
Roy Armstrong.

SUPPORTING CAST:
BRIAN BAIRD
– Matthew Costello
VICTOR BAIRD
– James Cosmo
PAULINE BAIRD
– Kathryn Howden
JOE HIGGISON
– Martin McCardie
, ROBERT HIGGISON
– Harry Jones
DOLLY ARMSTRONG
– Annie Raitt
ROY ARMSTRONG
– Martyn Hesford
TIBOR MERAY
– John Grillo
ANNE FAIRLEY
– Alison Peebles
WALTER FAIRLEY
– Stuart McGugan
DOUG KNOWLES
– John Murtagh
JULIAN SHARP
– James Cairncross
ANDY COCHRANE
– William McBain
PETER MACKAY
– Steve Owen
BRODIE
– Graham Valentine

Transmission dates:
28 September
–12 October 1988
Writer: Glenn Chandler
Producer/director:
Peter Barber-Fleming

concludes that Peter Mackay, a sacked employee, has taken revenge by putting rat poison into Meray's products. Meray is later blackmailed and tries to apprehend the culprit by arranging a secret 'meet' on the Glasgow Underground. He tackles the wrong person. The real extortioner, Brodie, posing as a blind man, gives the game away by stepping round the two brawlers as he makes his escape. Taggart steps forward, places a hand on the blind man's shoulder and, with great glee, announces: 'You're nicked.' In fact, Brodie is merely an opportunist, not the poisoner. When contract engineer Andy Cochrane dies from rat poisoning, Taggart suspects that the source of contamination could be a shop run by husband and wife Walter and Anne Fairley. Cochrane used to shop there and his wife worked there part-time. Taggart's search for the poisoner causes him to take an interest in the Baird family. Newly married to Pauline, Brian Baird works for his father Victor's pest control company. Brian has been suffering from recurring nightmares in which he is being chased and his wife and baby are placed in extreme danger. Taggart senses Brian's edginess. Victor Baird discovers that Brian has been tampering with the firm's allocation of poison. The latest victim – although not fatally – is Walter Fairley, the poison being traced to a bag of sugar in his shop. Taggart is faced with a baffling list of suspects, including mother and son Dolly and Roy Armstrong, a pair of antiques 'knockers' who use antique dealer Julian Sharp as their 'fence'. Roy, who becomes increasingly interested in his eccentric mother's accumulated wealth, is also involved in shady business dealings with Doug Knowles, Andy Cochrane's former partner. Together they make and market fake bronzes. Dolly is addicted to chocolates and is spotted by the surveillance team buying some at the Fairley shop. It is chocolates which prove to be her downfall, for soon she is discovered dead in a cinema, poisoned, clutching an almost entirely consumed box. At least Taggart is able to cross one suspect off his list. The lucky break he needs comes when he discovers that Roy Armstrong, Robert Higgison and Doug Knowles all did jury service together. It transpires that they had each wanted to commit a perfect murder and had achieved their ends by means of a three-way conspiracy.

Root of Evil

The Lomaxes are a long-established family of loan sharks. The oldest brother, Ken, owns an Edinburgh night-club called Oasis. He is married to Helen, a ex-call girl who now manages the club. There is no love lost between her and his two brothers – Mick, who operates out of his own pub in Glasgow, and Willie, the youngest and roughest of the three. Willie is particularly upset by the activities of Frank Bell, a rival moneylender. He hires two thugs, Nicholas Frame and George McSherry, to poison Frank's greyhound, Satan. Over at Oasis, Mick and Willie are confronted by Bill Shires, a schoolteacher now married to Mick's ex-wife, Lana. Bill and Lana have custody of David, Mick's fifteen-year-old son, and are furious that the two Lomax brothers have been visiting him outside of the agreed hours. It is a situation which will not happen again, for the next morning, Willie's body is found in a Glasgow alley. He has been bludgeoned to death with an axe. Investigating the murder, Taggart and Jardine unearth a handkerchief, stitched with the Glasgow Garden

A bomb destroys the car of moneylender, Frank Bell.

Festival motif, near the corpse. It is soaked in blood and contains traces of pollen from the vine-leaved abutilon plant. A search of Willie's flat produces a tallybook of borrowers, but from this list of 200 possible suspects, Mick Lomax tells brother Ken that he is convinced Frank Bell is the murderer. Frame and McSherry, now effectively unemployed, offer their dubious services to Frank Bell, who rejects them out of hand. That night, they hurl Satan's corpse through Frank's bedroom window. At the Tron Theatre, director Paul Hunter reports that the axe has gone missing from his play 'Lizzie Borden and the Axe'. Jardine finds himself attracted to the leading actress, Julie Adamson. Robert Carrera, a member of a barbershop quartet appearing at the theatre, also seems to have more than a passing interest in Julie. Taggart is not the only policeman on the case – two detective sergeants from Glasgow's South Side, Scott and Hind, are investigating the whole moneylending operation. But it is Taggart who uncovers a vital lead. The blood-stained handkerchief is one of a limited edition distributed only to exhibitors and advertisers at the Garden Festival. But while Taggart sets out to trace the owner, Frank Bell is blown to pieces in his car outside the post office. Taggart and McVitie visit Ken Lomax, who is tending the plants in his greenhouse. The green-fingered McVitie observes that Ken has no vine-leaved abutilon plants. Jardine takes Julie for a coffee but whilst he is on the phone to Taggart, she mysteriously disappears. Soon the missing axe is returned to the theatre. A third moneylender meets a grisly end when Mick Lomax is axed to death in the doorway of his flat. Young David tries to implicate Bill Shires but his story is discredited. It also emerges that David gave a false alibi for Mick Lomax for the night before Frank Bell's death. It was Mick who murdered Bell. Still with two killings to solve, Taggart begins to probe a possible link between Helen Lomax and Julie Adamson, who is clearly distressed to read the report of Mick's demise. Eventually, Helen reveals that Julie had once been employed at Oasis. On her first night there, Julie claimed to have been raped by Willie and Mick and never returned. But in truth it was Scott and Hind who had raped her, and when the two rogue policemen corner her again on her houseboat, she is saved only by Jardine's timely arrival. Taggart fits the pieces of the jigsaw together: Robert Carrera is Julie's father. Mistakenly thinking that Willie and Mick Lomax had raped her, Carrera had set out to avenge his daughter's attack by murdering them. The abutilon plant is found adorning the stage at the Tron Theatre where Carrera was performing.

SUPPORTING CAST:
ALISON TAGGART
– Leigh Biagi
KEN LOMAX
– Kenny Ireland
MICK LOMAX
– John Kane
WILLIE LOMAX
– Gordon Kane
HELEN LOMAX
– Celia Imrie
MRS LOMAX
– Irene Sunters
JULIE ADAMSON
– Emma D'Inverno
ROBERT CARRERA
– Peter Kelly
BILL SHIRES
– Jonathan Hackett
LANA SHIRES
– Elizabeth Millbank
DAVID SHIRES
– Joseph McFadden
PAUL HUNTER
– Alan Vicary
NICHOLAS FRAME
– David Meldrum
GEORGE MCSHERRY
– Stewart Ennis
FRANK BELL
– Andrew Robertson
DET. SGT. SCOTT
– Tom Mannion
DET. SGT. HIND
– Don Gallagher

Double Jeopardy

Transmission date:
30 December 1988
Writer: Glenn Chandler
Executive producer:
Robert Love
Producer:
Peter Barber-Fleming
Director: Jim McCann

SUPPORTING CAST:
ROWENA BAIN
– Rose McBain
MAURICE BAIN
– James Laurenson
CAROL BAIN
– Valerie Gogan
PAM FLEMING
– Sheila Ruskin

Taggart and Jardine are called in to investigate the case of Rowena Bain, whose body is found in a wood. All outward appearances and forensic evidence suggest suicide. However, Rowena had made several appointments in her diary for the day she died, and it seems that she was looking forward to moving to Bavaria, where she planned to take over a country inn with her builder husband, Maurice, and daughter Carol. Taggart is suspicious, a view shared by Rowena's sister, Pam Fleming. She believes that Maurice also murdered his first wife, Leslie, and that Maurice and Carol (who is in fact only his step-daughter) are lovers. So when Maurice and Carol fly off to Munich as planned, Taggart decides to follow them. Taggart is convinced that Maurice killed Rowena because he was having an affair with Carol, but it emerges that Rowena really had committed suicide. However, she had deliberately made her death look suspicious in order to lay the blame on Maurice. For she knew that he had killed his first wife. Leslie's body is duly found walled up in Maurice Bain's old house.

Flesh and Blood

Transmission dates:
5–19 September 1989
Writer: Glenn Chandler
Producer: Robert Love
Director: Alan Macmillan

SUPPORTING CAST:
CHARLIE FORBES
– Andrew Byatt
JANIE ROSS
– Karen Westwood
MARTIN DUFFY
– Gerard O'Hare
TOM MCALLISTER
– Duncan Bell
GEORGE MCKNIGHT
– Roy Sampson
VIOLET MCKNIGHT
– Dorothy Paul
ANDREW MCKNIGHT
– Simon Donald
FERN MCCULLOCH
– Hilary Maclean

Martin Duffy, an Irishman living in Glasgow, and his friend, baker Tom McAllister, ambush a delivery van on its way to the Stranraer Ferry. Instead of finding video recorders, as expected, they uncover explosives. Fearing an Irish connection, McAllister wants nothing to do with them, but Duffy approaches expert safeblower George McKnight, who, after some initial hesitation, plans to use them to pull a 'million pound job' by blowing the safe of local millionaire Bernie Sullivan at his Hogmanay party. Taggart has attended the wedding of social worker Janie Ross and prisoner Charlie Forbes, who is serving time for theft. In the vaults beneath Glasgow University, Janie is engrossed in a complex role-playing game with her friends Fern McCulloch, Kevin Brown and Duncan Knox. During the course of this latest game, Janie's character, Valiara the Fighter, is killed. Janie leaves in despair, only to be crushed to death by a car in a quiet back street. A mysterious Irishman named Flynn traces Duffy, who protests that he came across the explosives by accident. Flynn allows the safe job to go ahead on the understanding that his organization will keep all the proceeds. Violet McKnight plans to spend Christmas in a country cottage with husband George and their adopted son, Andrew. The latter works as a cleaner at a health centre run by Dr Gilchrist, an attractive woman in her forties. The cottage is owned by Janie Ross's parents. After learning that Janie had dropped the cottage keys in to the McKnight home on the day of her death, Taggart and Jardine pay George a visit and almost stumble upon him and Duffy planning the safe job. But when the explosives go missing, Duffy fears retribution from Flynn. While Jardine tries to decipher the clues for a treasure hunt trail which Janie was laying for Boxing Day, Dr Gilchrist visits a wealthy recluse, Mrs Cameron, who lives in a large Victorian house, stuffed full of newspapers and cats. She had her child stolen from her when it was a baby. Taggart's quiet Christmas Day with Jean, Aunty Hettie and Aunty Peggy is interrupted when the McKnights' cottage is devastated by an explosion. Surely nobody could have survived it. Driving to the scene, Jardine realizes he is following exactly the route set out in Janie's treasure hunt. Detective Superintendent McVitie receives a visit from solicitor Harry McBean. He had a letter entrusted to him by George McKnight which was only to be opened after the death of both George and Violet. It states that Andrew is the kidnapped son of Mrs Cameron. Then Mrs Cameron is viciously murdered in her mansion. Andrew has a cast-iron alibi. Genetic fingerprinting proves that Andrew is not Mrs Cameron's son after all, and will therefore not inherit her fortune. It seems that a gamesmaster is at work. That man is George McKnight. He had not perished in the explosion, and had killed Janie Ross and Mrs Cameron because they were in danger of destroying his plot to make Andrew the heir to a fortune.

Love Knot

Taggart and Jardine are called to the Clyde, where a dredger has pulled out the corpse of a young woman. She has granite tethered to her wrists with climbing rope and her face is badly disfigured. Forensic evidence suggests that the weapon used was an ice-axe. The investigation leads the police to the North Face Club, a climbing club of which Susan Bryant, a physiotherapist in her late twenties, is unofficial secretary. She provides a list of club members but it transpires that she has omitted that of Russell Hendry, an ex-boyfriend, whom Jardine is unable to trace. A suitcase found in the river identifies the corpse as Elisabeth von Aschenberg, daughter of Countess Theresa von Aschenberg, a widowed Austrian aristocrat who now owns the Achnacrae Lodge Hotel in the Highlands. The Countess flies to Glasgow to identify the body and tells Taggart that Elisabeth had come to the city in response to an advertisement for a nanny placed in *The Scotsman* by a Mr Carnegie. The only person Elisabeth had known in Glasgow was Robby Meiklejohn, with whom she had conducted an affair until the two were separated by the Countess. Robby was not considered suitable, although he now works as barman at the Countess's hotel. Taggart and Jardine head north, spending the night in a traditional Highland bed and breakfast. A cramped bedroom, nylon sheets and lumpy porridge fuel Taggart's distaste for rural life. Jardine questions wealthy fish-farm owner Jack MacFarlane about his relationship with the dead girl. It is clear that she resented his attentions to her mother. Taggart and Jardine interview Robby, but a well-supported alibi proves that he was climbing in the Lake District at the time of the murder. A stranger has watched the Countess arrive home and finds a note addressed to Mr Carnegie on his tent, inviting him to a rendezvous. Later that night, the stranger is axed to death in his

DUNCAN KNOX
– Stuart Davids
KEVIN BROWN
– Alastair Galbraith
FLYNN
– Tony Rohr
BERNIE SULLIVAN
– Jimmy Logan
DR GILCHRIST
– Jane Nelson Peebles
MRS CAMERON
– Margo Cunningham
HARRY MCBEAN
– Bill Deniston

(Previous page): Taggart, Jardine and two police marksmen lie in wait for the fleeing Flynn.

Transmission date:
1 January 1990
Writer: Glenn Chandler
Executive producer:
Robert Love
Producer/director: Peter
Barber-Fleming

SUPPORTING CAST:
COUNTESS VON ASCHENBERG
– Jenny Runacre
JACK MACFARLANE
– David Robb
SUSAN BRYANT
– Shauna Baird
ROBBY MEIKLEJOHN
– John Michie
JASON
– Ewan Bremner
RUSSELL HENDRY
– Lawrence Ventry

tent. The note is signed 'Elisabeth' but a check against a sample of Elisabeth's handwriting shows that it is not hers. However, her writing does match the letter placing the advertisement in *The Scotsman*. Mr Carnegie does not exist – he was a figment of Elisabeth's imagination. The Countess is confused by this deceit and admits to overhearing several telephone calls between Elisabeth and someone using coded language. She had thought it was simply Elisabeth and Robby trying to meet without her knowledge. Now she is not so sure. A further interview with Robby leads Taggart to the conclusion that the murdered stranger was Russell Hendry, Susan Bryant's former boyfriend. Hendry's most recent girlfriend was Elisabeth von Aschenberg. The jealous Bryant had been driven to kill and had enlisted the help of a rock-climbing toy boy, Jason.

Hit-and-run murderer Kenneth Rose has much to look anxious about.

Transmission dates:
22 February 1 and
8 March 1990
Writers: Glenn Chandler,
Stuart Hepburn
Producer: Robert Love
Director: Haldane Duncan

SUPPORTING CAST:
JOHN GREENEY
– Neil McKinven
LESLEY HAY
– Aline Mowat
GEORGE HAY
– Joe Dunlop
JOANNA GILLAN
– Jan Carey
DONALD GILLAN
– Ian McCulloch
DAVID CRAWFORD
– Paul Higgins
JAMES LITTLE
– Robert McIntosh
SAM PARIS
– James Carroll Jordan
KENNETH ROSE
– James Telfer

Hostile Witness

David Crawford, a young man living in a high-rise flat, strangles his wife and tries to cover his tracks by making it look like the work of a maniac. The thought of a Ripper-type killer on the loose in Glasgow in the Year of Culture does not please Taggart. Meanwhile, at the local by-election, Jean Taggart is a candidate on behalf of A Better Deal for the Disabled. Among her opponents is Joanna Gillan, standing for the Referendum for the Return of Capital Punishment Party. Sadly, she has close experience of the subject since her first husband, a police inspector, was murdered some years previously while attempting to prevent a building society robbery. Her brother-in-law, antique bookseller George Hay, is acting as her agent, but strangely neither her present husband, airline pilot Donald, nor her sister Lesley show any enthusiasm for the campaign. Indeed, Lesley is more interested in pursuing her affair with Sam Paris, a young American from the naval base at Holy Loch. Suddenly a man called John Greeney confesses to the murder of Mrs Crawford. He is quickly revealed as a time-waster, but his wrong description of the victim's footwear triggers a thought in Taggart's mind. Under interrogation, David Crawford breaks down and admits to the killing. The case is solved. Next Greeney confesses to the murder of a young lad whose body is found in a ditch on the outskirts of the city. Taggart gives him short shrift and the true culprit is found to be shop owner Kenneth Rose. Before Taggart can arrest him, Rose hangs himself. The election campaign continues apace, although Joanna and Donald quarrel about the amount of time she is spending on it. At a public meeting, she faints as she is about to make her speech. George offers to drive her home. The following morning, some workmen find George's van parked at a spot popular with courting couples. Inside, lying side by side, are the bodies of Joanna Gillan and George Hay. They have each been shot twice through the head. Greeney, who works at Little's, the printers where Joanna's campaign leaflets were printed, wastes no time in confessing. Taggart wishes he could have *him* murdered! But Greeney is not finished yet and in the new candidate's campaign leaflets, inserts a 'confession' from a contract killer, hired by Lesley and Sam to get George out of the way. Before Taggart can act, Lesley and Sam are shot dead. It is a professional job. The first question that springs to Taggart's mind is, did the hitman employed by Lesley and Sam to kill George and Joanna then turn on his employers to prevent them from talking? The murder of Lesley and Sam is one to which Greeney does not confess. He has other things on his mind – James Little has sacked him and he has been thrown out of his digs. Taggart begins to wonder whether there is a connection with the old building society murder, and the pressures of the case mean that he arrives at the polling station just too late to vote for Jean. She is not amused. Taggart's hunch is right, though. The robber who shot the policeman in the building society raid turns out to be James Little. He had subsequently been killing off all potential witnesses. He manages to evade Taggart by hiding in a removal lorry, only for it to be shunted away to a container depot, leaving its human cargo to rot inside.

Evil Eye

(See Chapter 6 'THE MARYHILL FILES' page 66)

Death Comes Softly

Ronnie and Lillias Blacklock fail in their efforts to persuade her father, Fred Scott, who lives alone, to go into a home for two weeks while they are away on holiday. In their absence, an assailant smothers him with a pillow in his bed. Taggart and Jardine have been giving evidence in court. The defending advocate is Alistair Balmain and among those in the public gallery is Lena Henderson, an elderly lady who lives with Sophie McQueen, Balmain's devoted aunt. At the post office, the same one used by Mr Scott, Lena Henderson

Advocate Alistair Balmain.

collects two pensions. She is served by Donald King, who slips her a £10 note out of his own pocket. It becomes apparent that Mr Scott was fond of a bargain and paid great attention to the advertisements on the noticeboard. The adverts lead Taggart to a Commander Gunner, RN, a spiritual healer who had been seen visiting Mr Scott. Since Balmain is about to sell the house, he puts Aunt Sophie in a home, where she quickly befriends Noel Brown. The young man clearing the tables at the home is Pete McCulloch, Donald King's colleague at the post office. With Sophie away, Lena Henderson is left alone in the house. As Lena lies asleep that night, a pillow is pushed into her face. In his room at the home, Mr Brown suggests to Commander Gunner, who is treating Mrs Brown, that he may need to help Sophie with spiritual healing following the loss of her friend. Sophie will have none of it. Sophie tells Taggart that Lena used to be a blackmailer. The entries in the dead woman's notebook indicate that she may have received money from a Mr

Transmission dates:
3–17 December 1990
Writer: Julian Jones
Executive producer:
Robert Love
Producer:
Murray Ferguson
Director: Laurence Moody

SUPPORTING CAST:
WPC JACKIE REID
– Blythe Duff
ALISTAIR BALMAIN
– David Rintoul
SOPHIE MCQUEEN
– Eve Pearce
LENA HENDERSON
– Georgine Anderson
RONNIE BLACKLOCK
– Bill Leadbitter

Mackenzie on the day she died. Piece by piece, Bruce Mackenzie is tracked down. He had been a defence witness at his brother's trial and Lena had caught him trying to influence jurors. During the night, Pete McCulloch is woken by screaming. Mr Brown had apparently entered Sophie's room by mistake. Taggart takes Pete in for questioning and learns that Donald was being blackmailed by Lena over an undeclared conviction for forgery. Two teenage girls, Pauline and Fiona, help Balmain clear out his aunt's house. In the loft, they find an old trunk – and inside it, a mummified body. The body turns out to be that of Sophie's previous lodger, Winifred Forsyth. Sophie tells the girls that she murdered 'Winnie' and asks them to fetch her a large bottle of aspirin. They refuse and leave as Balmain arrives. Later that night, Sophie too is suffocated in her sleep. When Taggart and Jardine discover that Sophie also knew Commander Gunner, suspicion falls on him. But then Taggart sets a trap and ensnares Pauline and Fiona. Their motive for the murders? Nothing more than killing for kicks.

Rogues' Gallery

(See Chapter 6 'THE MARYHILL FILES' page 77)

Taggart vists Professor Hutton's laboratory.

Transmission dates:
9–23 January 1992
Writer: Glenn Chandler
Producer: Robert Love
Director:
Graham Theakston

SUPPORTING CAST:
ANNIE GILMOUR
– Ann Mitchell
MORAG NEILSON
– Lorna Heilbron
DR DOUGLAS NEILSON
– Ken Drury
DEREK AMLOT
– Michael Cochrane

Nest of Vipers

When two skulls are unearthed close to a recent archaeological find, Taggart's immediate concern is whether one of them might be that of Janet Gilmour, a DHSS clerk who disappeared four years ago and whose body has never been found. In the intervening years, Taggart has remained in touch with the girl's mother, Annie, to the point of developing a friendship. Dr Andrews suggests that the skulls be given to Glasgow University's Professor Peter Hutton, a man with the ability to reconstruct faces. The story gets into the press and, shortly afterwards, the skulls are stolen from Hutton's laboratory. It would appear that someone does not want the skulls identified, although, on this occasion, a mistake by Hutton's young assistant has meant that the thief has inadvertently taken the Roman skulls instead. Over at a pharmaceutical firm, brilliant scientist Douglas Neilson is working on the extraction of venom from poisonous snakes and spiders as part of his research into anti-venoms. His talent is such that he is being head-hunted by a rival firm, much to the consternation of his wife, Morag. She has no intention of leaving Glasgow for fear that it will put an end to her affair with her husband's boss, Derek Amlot. As reports on the skulls suggest that one could be that of Janet Gilmour, the research laboratory is broken into and several deadly snakes and some poisonous funnel-web spiders are stolen. At a Burns Supper, Hutton is suddenly taken ill, the victim of a spider bite. The anti-venom fails to work and Hutton dies. Taggart sends Jardine and Reid to the lab party in the hope that they might pick up something useful. Among those present are Colin Murphy, a former colleague of Dr Neilson, who now works at the city zoo's reptile house, and Christine Gray, Neilson's assistant. These two take a drunken Neilson home, leaving him at the front door. As he slumps into bed, he is bitten by a deadly black mamba snake secreted between the sheets. It was one of those stolen from the laboratory. At last, Hutton's assistant completes one of the faces, and when Annie Gilmour sees it, she immediately identifies it as Janet. Christine Gray thinks of resigning, but is persuaded by Amlot and Maureen McDonald, the research director, to think it over. That evening, while entertaining Jardine, Christine goes to the kitchen to feed her dog and is bitten by a snake lying coiled up inside the sack of dog food. Again, the anti-venom does not work and Christine dies. By now, the second face is complete. Maureen McDonald recognizes it as that of Mary Hulme, a girl she interviewed for a job a couple of years previously. But Mary never turned up for work – it was assumed she had simply returned home to New Zealand. Maureen becomes the next victim when a venomous snake is left in her car as she collects her children from school. This puzzling scenario is solved when Taggart learns where Mary Hulme had lodged when she was in Glasgow for her interview. Taggart identifies the killer as Colin Murphy. He is a necrophiliac who, after murdering Janet Gilmour, had then silenced anyone who was in danger of uncovering his dreadful secret.

DR MAUREEN MCDONALD
– Juliet Cadzow
CHRISTINE GRAY
– Leone Connery
COLIN MURPHY
– Dougray Scott
PROF. PETER HUTTON
– Jeremy Young

Double Exposure

Lisanne Archer, whose husband George is in Barlinnie prison for theft, and Danny Lal are the only remaining occupants at the top of a run-down tenement block. They live in separate flats and are under constant harassment. Danny complains about the threats to lawyer Phillip McLean at the local resource centre. McLean and his partner, Eric Barr, appear to have serious business problems. To complicate McLean's life, he is torn between two women – his wife, Margaret, and Asian social worker Sharon Lal, sister of Danny. While much of Glasgow is preoccupied with the 'Old Firm' match between Celtic and Rangers at Parkhead, Phillip McLean is found dead in his car. It looks like suicide until the pathologist's report indicates murder. Barr seems to have the perfect alibi – a police video shows that he was at Parkhead throughout the match. Freelance photographer Diane Johnstone, who covered the big match and is helping Jean Taggart compile an accessibility pamphlet for the disabled, promises to deliver Barr a photograph she took of him some time ago. She is seduced by his charm. Meanwhile, a witness tells Taggart that Phillip McLean was last seen arguing heatedly with an Asian man, and the police set out to track down the elusive Danny Lal. The harassment continues against Lisanne, driving her to commit suicide by slitting her own throat. The Press distort the facts and George Archer, thinking Danny is responsible for his

Billy Friel is in no mood to hang around with Danny Lal and George Archer.

Transmission dates:
**30 January
–13 February 1992**
Writer: Stuart Hepburn
Executive producer:
Robert Love
Producer:
Murray Ferguson
Director: Gordon Flemyng

wife's death, escapes from prison. It emerges that Sharon Lal is pregnant by Phillip McLean, and that McLean was involved in a fraud which relied on removing Danny and Lisanne from the tenement block. Another implicated party is property developer Joe Malcolmson, a friend of Superintendent McVitie. Malcolmson's body is found at the meat market. Billy Friel, who had been watching Lisanne, ransacks Diane's flat. He tries to destroy all of her negatives but is disturbed before he can complete the task. He leaves a message explaining his failure on an answerphone. The answerphone belongs to the killer, Eric Barr. He wanted Diane's negatives destroyed because he feared someone would realize that it was not him at the 'Old Firm' game at all, but his twin brother. Eric Barr's final act before capture is to murder his twin.

Violent Delights

(See Chapter 6 'THE MARYHILL FILES' page 87)

The Hit Man

In 1981, a series of payroll snatches ended when the robbers' car crashed, killing the driver, a young woman called Sharon, and seriously injuring an innocent passer-by, Louise Wilkie. Ten years on, Sharon's daughter, Ailsa Catto, is the spoilt child of Tommy Catto, owner of a successful group of Scottish hotels, but Louise Wilkie is permanently hospitalized, to the chagrin of husband George. Shortly before Tommy's marriage to Mary, a former accounts clerk with Catto's Hotels, his elder brother, Jimmy, is released from prison at the end of a twenty-year sentence. Jimmy, an old schoolmate of Taggart, went on to earn a living as a notorious hit man. Among the guests at the wedding are two of Tommy's pals, businessmen David Laing and Malcolm Steen, Ailsa's boyfriend, Gary, and the unseen George Wilkie, who expresses his bitterness by spraying the word 'Criminals' all over the Catto Range Rover. A few days later, Tommy, Jimmy, Ailsa, Laing and Steen fly to Tarbert for a fishing trip. Just before the return journey to Glasgow, Ailsa is taken ill, leaving Tommy to fly home alone. On the way, he suffers hallucinations after taking a drink from a flask. The plane crashes and Tommy is killed instantly. The death was no accident. Jardine suspects Jimmy Catto, but Taggart remains sceptical. It becomes apparent that Mary, Tommy's new wife, is still having an affair with her former boss, Catto's Hotels' Director of Finance, Macnally. Since she and Mary will now inherit the hotel chain, Ailsa meets Macnally to learn something of the business. As she leaves she is cornered by a gunman dressed as a priest. He tells her that she is to continue with 'the deal' – just like her father. Ailsa tells Jimmy about her terrifying experience so he visits his old supplier, Billy Boyce, to ask him for a gun. Billy refuses and the following day is found shot through the head, his face covered with a white handkerchief – Jimmy's trademark. While Jimmy denies any part in the killing, Mary receives a visit from the mysterious 'priest'. Ailsa sees him leave and follows him to the yard of Steen's plant hire company. Working late at the yard, Steen is shot through the head. His henchman, the 'priest', meets the same fate. They had been killed with the same gun that was used on Billy Boyce. A frightened Jimmy goes into hiding. He breaks cover to phone Taggart, suggesting that the key to the killings is to be found in the hotel group's affairs, which may be linked to the payroll robberies of the early 1980s. The murderers turn out to be Ailsa and Gary, the motive sheer greed so that she could get her hands on her father's business.

Fatal Inheritance

When Caroline Kemp is stabbed to death in the driveway of her workplace, the Napier Health Resort, her employer, Dr Janet Napier, stands trial for murder. Taggart is convinced of Janet Napier's guilt, principally because her husband, Gerald, was having an affair with Caroline, but the jury return a verdict of 'not

Doctors Gerald and Janet Napier.

proven'. Janet subsequently returns to the health farm which Gerald, their daughter Belinda and son Jeremy have been running in her absence. Gerald, who suspects that his wife did kill Caroline, plans to move out. Taggart is so infuriated by the verdict that McVitie orders him to take a couple of weeks' rest. Jean, delighted at the prospect of having him home for once, thinks a spot of decorating could be therapeutic, but Taggart has other ideas. Unbeknown to McVitie, he decides to take his rest at the Napiers' health farm. The Napier family are uneasy at his presence, as is a new member of staff, Ian Gowrie. Taggart

Transmission date:
1 January 1993
Writer: Glenn Chandler
Producer: Robert Love
Director: Alan Macmillan

SUPPORTING CAST:
DR JANET NAPIER
– Hannah Gordon
DR GERALD NAPIER
– Francis Matthews
BELINDA NAPIER
– Caroline Hunnisett
JEREMY NAPIER
– Scott Cleverdon
IAN GOWRIE
– Henry Ian Cusick
JOHN HELLIWELL
– Jamie Roberts

learns that some of the guests form an escape committee and sneak out to the nearby pub, where they are warmly greeted by John, the landlord. Then a series of anonymous letters calling Janet a murderess prompts Gerald to call in the police, and Jardine and Reid arrive. They are amazed to discover Taggart – they had thought he had gone on holiday with Jean. Taggart's secret is finally exposed when Jean phones McVitie to complain that her husband is still working. McVitie explodes but Taggart, true to form, refuses to budge. The peace of the resort is shattered when Belinda, returning from a night out with her father in Glasgow, is murdered in similar circumstances to those surrounding the death of Caroline Kemp. Taggart remembers that Caroline had borrowed Belinda's car that night. Was Belinda really the intended victim and has the killer waited for another opportunity? In any case, Taggart concludes that Janet Napier must be innocent after all. She tells him how, many years ago, she had been forced to flee South Africa after accidentally killing a young girl, Rhona Helliwell, by giving her an overdose of insulin. The suggestion that the dead girl's father could have harboured thoughts of revenge gathers momentum when it transpires that the Helliwells had returned to their native Scotland a year or two after their daughter's death. But both parents are now dead (the mother committed suicide) and the other child, a son, was taken into care. Then Gerald Napier is murdered, also with a deeply inflicted knife wound in the back. Janet is certain that someone is trying to destroy her entire family. She is right – and the culprit is John, the friendly landlord. His real surname is Helliwell. He is the long-lost brother of the tragic Rhona.

Killer Albert Newman proves a tough nut for Taggart to crack.

Transmission dates:
8–22 October 1992
Writer: Stuart Hepburn
Executive producer:
Robert Love
Producer:
Murray Ferguson
Director: Mike Vardy

SUPPORTING CAST:
ALISON BAIN
– Sara Stewart
ALISTAIR HOGG
– Sandy Welch
ALBERT NEWMAN
– John Bluthal
MAURICE NEWMAN
– David Lyon
JAMIE O'HARE
– David Herlihy
BARRY RICHARDS
– Billy Hartman
EDDIE RICHARDS
– Paul Sykes
MARJORIE RICHARDS
– Lindy Whiteford
MARTINE EVANS
– Sian Thomas
PETER BRENTON
– Mark Markham
RUSSELL BRYCE
– Laurie Ventry

Ring of Deceit

The murder of research scientist Julie Smith, her body dumped on a refuse tip, is believed to be the latest work of a serial rapist known as 'The Mechanic'. She had been abducted at night at an unmanned railway station. The case attracts the attention of ambitious television presenter Alison Bain, who, despite opposition from her producer, Martine Evans, and co-presenter, Alistair Hogg, intends devoting an entire edition of the live current affairs programme, *Crisis Point*, to the plight of women and violence. She lures Jardine on to the show, departs from the agreed line of questioning and gives him a hard time. An early suspect is Jewish jeweller Maurice Newman, caught acting strangely by his father, Albert. Alumina, a grinding agent in gem cutting, was found under the dead girl's fingernails and Maurice has scratches on his face. He was also spotted arguing with a woman in his car near the scene of Julie's death on the night of the murder. But the 'woman' turns out to be Maurice's male lover, student Peter Brenton. And when Julie's boss reveals that she had been working with alumina in her laboratory, the case against Maurice collapses. Meanwhile, small-time haulage contractor Jamie O'Hare has been recording on video the operations of a much more successful company run by Barry and Marjorie Richards. Barry and his brother Eddie are convinced that Jamie is out to sabotage their business. Eddie reacts by demolishing Jamie's caravan. Jamie then telephones Alison Bain, promising her some information which is 'dynamite', but at the pre-arranged meeting place he is shot by an unseen assailant. He dies later in hospital. While Alistair Hogg consults a private detective, seemingly to investigate a Nazi war crime, Taggart and McVitie agree to using police officers as decoys in an attempt to trap the killer. The undercover operation proves fruitless but on her way home that evening, Reid is attacked by 'The Mechanic'. Her assailant is train guard Russell Bryce. He is 'The Mechanic' – the man who killed Julie Smith – but not the killer of Jamie O'Hare. When Alistair Hogg is also murdered, the trail leads to old Albert Newman. During the war, Albert had saved his skin by acting as a Nazi collaborator, using his knowledge of the jewellery trade to remove the gold from prisoners' teeth. Hogg had found about his activities and was threatening to expose him. Albert feared that O'Hare also knew too much. Both had to be silenced.

Death Benefits

(See Chapter 6 'THE MARYHILL FILES' page 97)

Gingerbread

Private investigator Tom Barrow is playing with his children Simon, 12, and Nicola, 8, in woodland close to a cottage owned by Betty Duncan, a widow in her sixties. Tom returns to the cottage that evening for a clandestine meeting, but later that night is butchered in his own home with a razor by a caped intruder. The gruesome scene is witnessed by young Simon. Taggart's investigations take him to Edinburgh and a meeting with Detective Chief Inspector Gault, who explains that Barrow was trying to trace Philip Chalmers, the missing

Widow Betty Duncan holds a sinister secret behind her sweet facade.

husband of Elsa Chalmers. The Barrow children are put into emergency foster care, looked after by Willie and Jessie Fraser, who share a house with magician and children's entertainer, Albert Brockwell. Returning from a short holiday, Elsa Chalmers finds a message on her answerphone. It is Tom Barrow's dying words – something about checking 'gingerbread men'. Simon is sure his father's death is connected with the cottage in the woods. Nobody believes him, so he decides to explore for himself and comes face to face with Betty Duncan, armed with an axe. Far from trying to harm him, she asks him to return for tea. In a rough Glasgow bar, Jimmy Buchanan celebrates his bingo winnings in the company of prostitutes Jenny McClusky and Ann Kirk. Jenny is young and vulnerable, Ann is older and badly scarred. He leaves with Jenny but that night is murdered at Betty Duncan's cottage. Jimmy Buchanan's disappearance seems to match the pattern of other missing persons. Could a serial killer be involved? A dog uncovers a severed hand. It is identified as belonging to Philip Chalmers. Jardine breaks off from his romance with crime writer Gemma Normanton to help in the interviews with the two prostitutes. Later, on her way to meet a client called Ginger, Jenny McClusky telephones the police with what she thinks is vital information. Before she can deliver a message, her throat is slit by a caped figure. That same night, Albert Brockwell arrives home late. While being entertained for tea, Simon Barrow had noticed a cape behind the door of Betty Duncan's cottage. It looked like the one his father's killer wore. Later, he sneaks back to investigate further. Betty surprises him and, herself terrified, tells him never to return. For she knows the identity of the killer – it is her daughter, Ann Kirk, who has been murdering clients in revenge for being horribly scarred by one years earlier. She killed them after luring them back to her mother's cottage. It was Betty Duncan, also a former prostitute, who had found that fateful client, and before Taggart brings her spree to an end Ann Kirk makes sure that her mother too pays for her sins.

Death Without Dishonour

Nicky O'Donnell has lain in a coma since the night the taxi she was driving for her father, Sean, was attacked. The incident led to the escalation of a taxi war between

Transmission dates:
20 April–4 May 1993
Writer: Glenn Chandler
Executive producer:
Robert Love
Producer:
Murray Ferguson
Director: Sarah Hellings

SUPPORTING CAST:
BETTY DUNCAN
– Mary MacLeod
SIMON BARROW
– Gary Hollywood
GEMMA NORMANTON
– Fiona Gillies
NICOLE BARROW
– Heather Foster
ALBERT BROCKWELL
– Christopher Robbie
ELSA CHALMERS
– Vivien Heilbron
DCI BOBBY GAULT
– Hugh Fraser
WILLIE FRASER
– Malcolm Rennie
JESSIE FRASER
– Sheila Reid
ANN KIRK
– Anne-Marie Timoney
TOM BARROW
– Jay Smith
JENNY MCCLUSKY
– Alice Bree
JIMMY BUCHANAN
– Andrew Melville

erstwhile partners Peter Strachan and Sean O'Donnell, as a result of which the latter is now standing trial for conspiracy to murder and arson. The prosecution is being conducted by the feisty Michelle Duncan, a beautiful and highly ambitious advocate, who, with Taggart's help, has persuaded Strachan to give evidence, in return for a guarantee of safe custody for him and his son Tony. In the middle of the court case, two men arrive in Glasgow. Handsome young Australian musician Bill Hamilton is on his way to the Grand Ole Opry to audition for country and western singer Carlson Stewart. En route, he bumps into Alison Taggart and agrees to play piano at the opening of the wine bar she is running with new boyfriend Matt Dillon. A more sinister arrival is hit man Joseph Durrant. Hired by O'Donnell, he proceeds to blast Strachan's taxi office to pieces with a sawn-off shotgun. In the wake of a fight with O'Donnell's vodka-soaked wife, Deedee, his boutique-owning mistress Liz Galbraith also finally offers to give evidence for the prosecution. Tony Strachan and his father argue about the increasing violence – it was Tony who was responsible for the attack on Nicky O'Donnell. Peter Strachan wants to call a truce with O'Donnell. Next day in court, Michelle Duncan goes missing. She is eventually located in the cell area, strangled by a length of wire. Everyone becomes jumpy, not least star witnesses Peter Strachan and Liz Galbraith. When Jardine goes to check on Strachan, the guards say that he is upstairs taking a bath. All seems normal – until water seeps through the kitchen ceiling. Strachan is found dead in the bath, a wire pulled tight around his neck. Taggart is furious – a vital witness murdered while under police protection. While Durrant makes an attempt to get at Liz Galbraith, Tony Strachan takes the law into his own hands and takes a pot shot at O'Donnell and his henchman, Liam Patrick. Durrant has been secretly camping out on land owned by farmer Derek Kennedy, and it is Kennedy who reveals what could be the missing link in the case. Kennedy, Michelle Duncan and Peter Strachan were all in the Gulf War Reserve. During a search of Michelle's belongings, Jardine and Reid find a list of people who were together at the time of the Gulf War. Eight of the names are underlined in red – including those of Kennedy and Strachan. Soon there are two more murders – Stuart Barbour and Kennedy – and Taggart is becoming increasingly anxious at the amount of time his daughter is spending with Bill Hamilton. He has good reason to worry since it soon becomes apparent that Bill Hamilton is the killer. His brother had been goaded and accused of cowardice by a group of soldiers for refusing to go to the Gulf. They had made him walk along a narrow parapet from where he fell to his death. They had not meant to kill him – but that was of no concern to Bill, who set out to avenge his brother's death by murdering all those involved.

Alison Taggart hits the right note with Bill Hamilton.

Transmission dates:
11–25 May 1993
Writer: Barry Appleton
Executive producer:
Robert Love
Producer: Paddy Higson
Director: Alan Macmillan

SUPPORTING CAST:
ALISON TAGGART
– Leigh Biagi
BILL HAMILTON
– Peter O'Brien
JOSEPH DURRANT
– David Schofield
MICHELLE DUNCAN
– Julie Peasgood
MATT DILLON
– Andy McEwan
SEAN O'DONNELL
– Ian McElhinney
DEEDEE O'DONNELL
– Eileen Pollock
PETER STRACHAN
– Billy Riddoch
TONY STRACHAN
– Ronnie McCann
LIAM PATRICK
– John Paul Connolly
LIZ GALBRAITH
– Victoria Burton
CARLSON STEWART
– Gilly Gilchrist
DEREK KENNEDY
– Jimmy Chisholm

Instrument of Justice

Gang member Sean Brady has decided to turn Queen's Evidence against his former boss, John McLintock, but the convoy taking the supergrass to court is ambushed by McLintock's men. Although Brady manages to escape, the incident proves a huge embarrassment to the authorities, not least newly promoted DCS Ellen Gordon and Procurator-Fiscal Ian Rattray. To Taggart's disgust, DCS Gordon brings in Superintendent Brand and DI Gemmill, complaints and discipline officers from Edinburgh, to investigate a possible leak of information to McLintock's gang about Brady's route to court. The source of the leak turns out to be Alan Forrester, a young lawyer on Rattray's staff. Forrester has been having an affair with Rattray's wife, Lady Sarah, and is in McLintock's pocket. When Forrester and Rattray's secretary, Suzanne Harris, arrive for work in the morning, they discover the corpse of security guard Billy Connor obstructing the lift doors. In the Procurator-Fiscal's office lies the body of Ian Rattray. The presence of Brady's fingerprints in the office put him high on the list of suspects, along with Neil Howden, one of McLintock's cohorts. Another set of prints is also discovered. The prints belong to suspected sex offender Dennis Gilmour. But it becomes known that Gilmour and the deceased Connor are the same person. Meanwhile Forrester, after being threatened by Howden, is butchered in his flat. The murder weapon, a slater's rip, ties in with Alec Harris, Suzanne's father. He confesses to all the murders, but Taggart is sceptical. Is the father trying to protect the daughter, who is carrying Ian Rattray's baby? Still trying to flush out the elusive Brady, Howden and his partner Tam McLeod snatch schoolgirl Debbie Pearson, Brady's niece. When Brady shows up for a boatyard rendezvous, Howden shoots him. He falls backwards into the water, apparently dead. DCS Gordon, who is adamant that McLintock's men are behind the killings, tries to make her peace with Taggart. It would seem that she too is in danger, when a threatening message is found scrawled across her garage wall. Alec Harris is freed and in the continued absence of chief witness Brady, McLintock is also released from custody. But Brady dramatically surfaces to mow down McLintock and Howden outside the courtroom. He had survived the previous attack by wearing a flak jacket. Finally cornered, Brady maintains that he had nothing to do with the earlier murders, claiming that Rattray was already dead when he found him. Brady turns his gun on Jardine but is shot in the head by a police marksman. As far as McVitie is concerned, with Brady, McLintock and Howden dead, the Rattray case is closed. However, Taggart is not convinced and when Lady Sarah finds an old parcel posted to her by Forrester, the contents lead Taggart to an unlikely killer. It turns out that DCS Gordon was being blackmailed by Gilmour. So she killed him, and when Ian Rattray caught her in the act, he too had to die. Later, Alan Forrester guessed that she was behind the murders and met a similar fate. She might have got away with it but for Taggart's dogged refusal to admit defeat.

Transmission dates:
**30 September
–14 October 1993**
Writer: **Russell Lewis**
Executive producer:
Robert Love
Producer:
Bernard Krichefski
Director:
Richard Holthouse

SUPPORTING CAST:
SIR IAN RATTRAY
– Finlay Welsh
LADY SARAH RATTRAY
– Sarah Collier
ALAN FORRESTER
– Duncan Bell
SEAN BRADY
– Tommy Boyle
JOHN MCLINTOCK
– Peter Kelly
DET. CHIEF SUPERINTENDENT
ELLEN GORDON
– Barbara Horne
NEIL HOWDEN
– Tom Mannion
SUZANNE HARRIS
– Margo Gunn
SUPERINTENDENT BRAND
– Ross Davidson
DET. INSP. GEMMILL
– Jim Twaddale
TAM MCLEOD
– Tommy Flanagan
BILLY CONNOR
– James Bryce
ALEC HARRIS
– Dave Anderson
DEBBIE PEARSON
– Claire Cairns

Jackie Reid
questions Cathy
Adams.

**Transmission date:
1 January 1994**
Writer: Glenn Chandler
Producer: Robert Love
Director: Mike Vardy

SUPPORTING CAST:
PETER LIVINGSTONE
– Neil Duncan
DET. CON. ROB GIBSON
– Gray O'Brien
DR COLIN MILLAR
– Tony Doyle
NURSE RUTH MILLAR
– Maureen O'Brien
CATHY ADAMS
– Hilary MacLean
MARTIN ADAMS
– Paul Goodwin
JOAN MATHIESON
– Phyllida Law
IAN MATHIESON
– Liam Brennan
TOM FLEMING
– John Stahl
MICHELLE GIBSON
– Sharon Small
ERNIE WATTS
– Bob Docherty
MRS MOORE
– Mary Boyle
MARTA LIVINGSTONE
– Marisa Benlloch

(Previous page):
McLintock's
henchmen, McLeod
and Howden, go
gunning for gangster
Sean Brady.

Forbidden Fruit

Joan Mathieson arrives in Glasgow to be present at the birth of her daughter Cathy's first child. A difficult woman by nature, she is outraged to learn that the baby has been conceived by donor insemination. After calling into question the manhood of her architect son-in-law Martin Adams, she behaves strangely when invited to the christening of another child, conceived via the same fertility clinic. The parents of this second child are young Detective Constable Rob Gibson and his wife, Michelle. Taggart, meanwhile, receives a visit from his old sparring partner, Peter Livingstone, who now runs his own security firm. Livingstone and his Portuguese wife, Marta, want the Taggarts to be godparents to their recently born son, Xavier. While Cathy Adams is out shopping, Joan stays at home, only to be murdered with one of her own knitting needles through the throat. Her body is found in the conservatory, where Martin houses his collection of exotic butterflies. Taggart is convinced it's a 'domestic', with the hot-headed Martin the chief suspect. In the course of giving Rob Gibson's child a blood transfusion, the hospital notices that the baby has a different blood group from his parents, a curiosity since Rob contributed his own semen. Gibson questions Dr Colin Millar, who runs the fertility clinic with his wife, Ruth, and it emerges that Millar is the father of Rob's child, plus about sixty other children, including Cathy and Martin Adams's baby and Xavier Livingstone. Taggart has the unenviable job of telling Peter Livingstone who his child's father really is. When the news gets out, a group of angry fathers besiege the Millar home. Livingstone is arrested and Gibson suspended for not warning the police about the intended attack. Still probing the Mathieson murder, the police interview Joan's youngest son, Ian, who works for his uncle, Tom Fleming, in a freelance gardening firm. Reid visits Joan Mathieson's home in Perthshire and meets her neighbour, Ernie Watts. He reveals that Joan was terrified of butterflies, and Reid discovers an old newspaper cutting about a boating tragedy in Fife. As Reid is about to leave the house, she realizes that someone has set the place on fire. When she goes to Ernie for help, she finds him dead in his bungalow. He too has been killed with a knitting needle. The newspaper cutting leads Reid to a Mrs Moore, who admits that the person who drowned was her husband. Shortly afterwards, Tom Fleming is murdered. Mrs Moore asks Reid to visit her again, but Reid and Jardine arrive to find that she has been silenced in the same way as the others. Dr Millar tries to drown himself, but is unable to go through with it. However, he forgets to destroy his would-be suicide note, which is later found by Ruth. It emerges that Dr Millar was a bigamist twice over, and when one of his ex-wives, Joan Mathieson, had turned up and recognized him, he knew he had to kill her and anybody else who was in danger of uncovering his past.